Attack

Sam Brannon

Written by Sam Brannon

Gospel Time Ministries

Dedication

I would like to dedicate this book to two Ministers; Audie Vaughan and Bill Rountree.

Audie Vaughan Preached the revival at Rocky Mountain Community Church in Stilwell, Okla, when I got saved at the age of 12.

To Bill Rountree, I began to Preach at 13. Bill Rountree has been my Pastor Since I was 13 and a Mentor as a young Pastor.

These two Men of God have been a great light to me.

Thank you, Audie Vaughan and Bill Rountree.

Acknowledgement

First off, I want to Acknowledge My Lord and Savior, Jesus Christ, for he is my inspiration. Second, I want to Acknowledge My Parents, L. D. and Wanda Brannon, for they taught me the ways of the Word of God.

Third I want to Acknowledge My wife, Rosa Brannon; we got married at 19. She has stuck with me all these years and for a Wonderful son, Patrick Brannon. I like to Acknowledge the Publishing team with KDP.

Thankfulness

I would Like to say Thank you to my two older Brothers, Preston, and Darren, and a Step Sister, Angie Scott; these three have always been by my side to encourage me to write. Angie went on to the Lord in 2022, and even then, she told me to keep writing. Once again, thank you all for your support.

Table of Contents

Forward

There are many books to read on the attack, but in this book, we will learn how to attack the enemy that has taken control of our spiritual ground.

We are in a war, a war for our souls. So how do we fight for our soul? In this book, I have explained what tactics Satan uses to attack us and how we can overcome these tactics and overcome the battles of life. So, without further ado, let us study and learn how to attack.

-Sam Brannon

Chapter 1 What is Attack?

Have you ever wondered what an attack means? Let us look at the word attack in Webster's dictionary. There are four definitions; The first definition is; to use force against in order to harm. The second definition is; to speak or write against. The third definition is; to undertake vigorously; the fourth definition is; to begin acting harmfully.

Wow! What a defining word attack, but it all means the same: to overtake.

The game football is a good example of the word attack. There are two teams; one team controls the football, and the other team must overtake the other to obtain the ball. The team must work together to obtain the football, keep the ball and go for the touchdown, thus making points to win the game of football. There are rules the teams must play by, a leader to lead, and a teacher to teach the game plan to obtain the football and move the ball to the expected goal.

Let us look at each definition of the word attack. Each definition has a deeper meaning.

The first definition is to use force against in order to cause harm. As we said in football, there must be a leader; in life, we have two leaders; there is the One true God, Jehovah, our creator. The other leader is Satan, a fallen angel. Using the football as an illustration, we are the football. Satan is the captain of one football team, and God is the other captain of the other team. There is but one winner of this game called football(life).

Therefore rejoice, ye heavens, and ye that dwell in them.

Woe to the inhabiters of the earth and of the sea! for the devil is come down unto you, having great wrath, because he knoweth that he hath but a short time.

Rev 12:12

We read that Satan knows he has a short time. Satan will take everyone he can to hell: but wait, there is a way to have life; Jesus said this, regarding the devil, our enemy, and Jesus giving life.

The thief cometh not, but for to steal, and to kill, and to destroy: I am come that they might have life, and that they might have it more abundantly.

John 10:10

By looking at this verse, we see the devil has come to steal your soul, destroy your life, and steal everything you have.

Jesus told us this in the book of John chapter 3; we will find that there is abundant life in Jesus Christ, the son of God.

For God so loved the world, that he gave his only begotten Son, that whosoever believeth in him should not perish, but have everlasting life.

John 3:16

For God sent not his Son into the world to condemn the world; but that the world through him might be saved.

John3:17

He that believeth on him is not condemned: but he that believeth not is condemned already, because he hath not believed in the name of the only begotten Son of God.

John 3:18

God gave us a plan, just as the football team has. God has a winning plan to overcome the enemy, and that plan is Jesus Christ, God's only begotten son. When we accept Jesus, we are given the power to overcome Satan through Jesus Christ. Through Jesus, Satan is defeated, and victory is achieved!

When we repent and confess that Jesus Christ is Lord, we are attacking the past sins of our life, thus, becoming born again.

The second definition is to speak or write against. To attack is to talk against; let us look at two kinds of One way of speaking is when a preacher is sent. Let us look at what the word says:

How then shall they call on him in whom they have not believed? and how shall they believe in him of whom they have not heard? and how shall they hear without a preacher?

Romans 10:14

And how shall they preach, except they be sent? As it is written, How beautiful are the feet of them that preach the gospel of peace, and bring glad tidings of good things!

Romans10:15

God will send a messenger to be a witness of Jesus Christ, to tell us how to attack sin. Jesus, the son of God, was sent to save the world from sin, not to leave us in our sins.

The second way of speaking is us, praying. Looking at

Matthew 17:14-21.

And when they were come to the multitude, there came to him a certain man, kneeling down to him, and saying,

Mat 17:14

Lord, have mercy on my son: for he is lunatick and sore vexed: for ofttimes he falleth into the fire, and oft into the water.

Mat 17:15

And I brought him to thy disciples, and they could not cure him.

Mat 17:16

Then Jesus answered and said, O faithless and perverse generation, how long shall I be with you? how long shall I suffer you? bring him hither to me.

Mat 17:17

And Jesus rebuked the devil, and he departed out of him: and the child was cured from that very hour.

Mat 17:18

Then came the disciples to Jesus apart, and said, Why could not we cast him out?

Mat 17:19

And Jesus said unto them, Because of your unbelief: for verily I say unto you, If ye have faith as a grain of mustard seed, ye shall say unto this mountain, Remove hence to yonder place; and it shall remove, and nothing shall be impossible unto you.

Mat 17:20

Howbeit this kind goeth not out but by prayer and fasting.

Mat 17:21

First, we must have faith. What is faith? Hebrews 11:1 tells us this, Now faith is the substance of things hoped for, the evidence of things not seen.

Hebrews 11:1

This is faith; when we believe in what we cannot see, and what we are praying for, we have faith. When it comes to pass, we see the evidence. Notice what Jesus said; this goeth not out but by prayer and fasting. Jesus had to get alone and pray; even though Jesus was God in the flesh, Jesus had to have strength. And straightway Jesus constrained his disciples to get into a ship and to go before him unto the other side, while he sent the multitudes away.

Mat 14:22

And when he had sent the multitudes away, he went up into a mountain apart to pray: and when the evening was come, he was there alone.

Mat 14:23

Jesus had to get alone to pray. Praying unto God the Father. Jesus knew he would have to face the cross for the atonement for the sins of the world.

Then cometh Jesus with them unto a place called Gethsemane, and saith unto the disciples, Sit ye here, while I go and pray yonder.

Mat 26:36

And he took with him Peter and the two sons of Zebedee and began to be sorrowful and very heavy.

Mat 26:37

Then saith he unto them, My soul is exceeding sorrowful, even unto death: tarry ye here, and watch with me.

Mat 26:38

And he went a little further and fell on his face, and prayed, saying, O my Father, if it be possible, let this cup pass from me: nevertheless not as I will, but as thou wilt.

Mat 26:39

You may be asking. What does this have to do with me speaking (praying)? It has everything to do with our faith. Jesus is our first fruit.

But now is Christ risen from the dead, and become the first fruits of them that slept.

1Cor 15:20

Just as Jesus got away to pray, we must get away to pray. It is only through Jesus we can attack Satan. We must speak in faith and belief. Jesus said, "to speak to the mountain." A mountain can be any problem; sickness, sin, family, finances, and so on. So, by speaking to the mountain, we are attacking the mountain in faith. Jesus prayed, and by his faith, he said,

He went away again the second time, and prayed, saying, O my Father, if this cup may not pass away from me, except I drink it, thy will be done.

Matt 26:42

So, by doing the will of the Holy Spirit, we will walk in the Father's will, and in doing so, we attack sin. Just as a football player

goes for the win, we must go for the win too, in our spiritual life.

Let us examine what Jesus said to do next. Jesus said, 'to fast.'

But why fasting? Fasting means to abstain from food. When we fast and pray, we draw closer to the Father, and we draw strength spiritually. At this point, I will say being a Pastor/Evangelist; I have found that if I eat before church and then before I preach that night, it is harder to preach. But if I do not eat, it is easier to minister or preach. Fasting makes it easier to pray. Prayer and fasting combined will make you stronger for the attack on the enemy.

The third definition. To undertake vigorously. Vigorously means to have the strength or to be strong.

In the world of football, athletes must train vigorously and diet every day to obtain their strength.

We as Christians need to practice living right every day. We must lay aside every weight and sin,

Wherefore seeing we also are compassed about with so great a cloud of witnesses, let us lay aside every weight, and the sin which doth so easily beset us, and let us run with patience the race that is set before us,

Heb 12:1

Looking unto Jesus the author and finisher of our faith; who for the joy that was set before him endured the cross, despising the shame, and is set down at the right hand of the throne of God.

Heb 12:2

By praying and fasting and laying aside every weight and sin, we are training vigorously and obtaining our strength to attack.

Definition four. To begin acting harmfully. You may be saying, preacher? a Christian is to live a peaceful life. Yes, you are right, but to live a peaceful life, we must attack the enemy in the spiritual world. Let us look at Matthew 10:34- 42

Think not that I am come to send peace on earth: I came not to send peace, but a sword.

Mat 10:34

For I am come to set a man at variance against his father, and the daughter against her mother, and the daughter-in-law against her

mother-in-law.

Mat 10:35

And a man's foes shall be they of his own household.

Mat 10:36

He that loveth father or mother more than me is not worthy of me: and he that loveth son or daughter more than me is not worthy of me.

Mat 10:37

And he that taketh not his cross, and followeth after me, is not worthy of me.

Mat 10:38

He that findeth his life shall lose it: and he that loseth his life for my sake shall find it.

Mat 10:39

He that receiveth you receiveth me, and he that receiveth me receiveth him that sent me.

Mat 10:40

He that receiveth a prophet in the name of a prophet shall receive a prophet's reward, and he that receiveth a righteous man in the name of a righteous man shall receive a righteous man's reward.

Mat 10:41

And whosoever shall give to drink unto one of these little ones a cup of cold water only in the name of a disciple, verily I say unto you, he shall in no wise lose his reward.

Mat 10:42

We are to attack sin with a sword. What is the sword?

For the word of God is quick, and powerful, and sharper than any two-edged sword, piercing even to the dividing asunder of soul and spirit, and of the joints and marrow, and is a discerner of the thoughts and intents of the heart.

Heb 4:12

The Word of God is the sword. This is why we need to study the word of God (KJV). By knowing the word of God, we can attack and cause harm to Satan and his Imps.

Chapter 2 Attack on the Enemy

To attack the enemy, we must know his tactics, St. Paul tells us in,

To whom ye forgive anything, I forgive also: for if I forgave anything, to whom I forgave it, for your sakes forgave I it in the person of Christ;

2Cor 2:10

Lest Satan should get an advantage of us: for we are not ignorant of his devices.

2Cor 2:11

By knowing the tactics, we must know where Satan comes from. Just like a football team studies its opponent and their play tactics, we must study our adversary to learn the enemy's tactics.

Where do we learn who he is and what he does? In the Word of God. I want to stress, how important the King James Version is. It is as close as we can get to the original scriptures of the Bible in English. Let us look at Satan's beginnings.

Isaiah 14:9-17

Hell from beneath is moved for thee to meet thee at thy coming: it stirreth up the dead for thee, even all the chief ones of the earth; it hath raised up from their thrones all the kings of the nations.

Isa 14:9

All they shall speak and say unto thee, Art thou also become weak as we? art thou become like unto us?

Isa 14:10

Thy pomp is brought down to the grave, and the noise of thy viols: the worm is spread under thee, and the worms cover thee.

Isa 14:11

How art thou fallen from heaven, O Lucifer, son of the morning! how art thou cut down to the ground, which didst weaken the nations!

Isa 14:12

For thou hast said in thine heart, I will ascend into heaven, I will exalt my throne above the stars of God: I will sit also upon the mount of the congregation, in the sides of the north:

Isa 14:13

I will ascend above the heights of the clouds; I will be like the most High.

Isa 14:14

Yet thou shalt be brought down to hell, to the sides of the pit.

Isa 14:15

They that see thee shall narrowly look upon thee, and consider thee, saying, Is this the man that made the earth to tremble, that did shake kingdoms;

Isa 14:16

That made the world as a wilderness, and destroyed the cities thereof; that opened not the house of his prisoners?

Isa 14:17

We find that his name is Lucifer, and he was an angel. An angel that had pride in his heart. Ezekiel also tells us this in chapters 28:1-19, chapter 31:15-18.

The word of the LORD came again unto me, saying.

Eze 28:1

Son of man, say unto the prince of Tyrus, Thus, saith the Lord GOD; Because thine heart is lifted up, and thou hast said, I am a God, I sit in the seat of God, in the midst of the seas; yet thou art a man, and not God, though thou set thine heart as the heart of God:

Eze 28:2

Behold, thou art wiser than Daniel; there is no secret that they can hide from thee:

Eze 28:3

With thy wisdom and with thine understanding thou hast gotten thee riches, and hast gotten gold and silver into thy treasures:

Eze 28:4

By thy great wisdom and by thy traffick hast thou increased thy riches, and thine heart is lifted up because of thy riches:

Eze 28:5

Therefore, thus saith the Lord GOD; Because thou hast set thine heart as the heart of God;

Eze 28:6

Behold, therefore, I will bring strangers upon thee, the terrible of the nations: and they shall draw their swords against the beauty of thy wisdom, and they shall defile thy brightness.

Eze 28:7

They shall bring thee down to the pit, and thou shalt die the deaths of them that are slain in the midst of the seas.

Eze 28:8

Wilt thou yet say before him that slayeth thee, I am God? but thou shalt be a man, and no God, in the hand of him that slayeth thee.

Eze 28:9

Thou shalt die the deaths of the uncircumcised by the hand of strangers: for I have spoken it, saith the Lord GOD.

Eze 28:10

Moreover, the word of the LORD came unto me, saying,

Eze 28:11

Son of man, take up a lamentation upon the king of Tyrus and say unto him, Thus saith the Lord GOD; Thou sealest up the sum, full of wisdom, and perfect in beauty.

Eze 28:12

Thou hast been in Eden the garden of God; every precious stone was thy covering, the sardius, topaz, and the diamond, the beryl, the onyx, and the jasper, the sapphire, the emerald, and the carbuncle, and gold the workmanship of thy tabrets and of thy pipes was prepared in thee in the day that thou wast created.

Eze 28:13

Thou art the anointed cherub that covereth, and I have set thee so: thou wast upon the holy mountain of God; thou hast walked up and down in the midst of the stones of fire.

Eze 28:14

Thou wast perfect in thy ways from the day that thou wast created, till iniquity was found in thee.

Eze 28:15

By the multitude of thy merchandise, they have filled the midst of thee with violence, and thou hast sinned: therefore, I will cast thee as profane out of the mountain of God: and I will destroy thee, O covering cherub, from the midst of the stones of fire.

Eze 28:16

Thine heart was lifted up because of thy beauty; thou hast corrupted thy wisdom by reason of thy brightness: I will cast thee to the ground, I will lay thee before kings, that they may behold thee.

Eze 28:17

Thou hast defiled thy sanctuaries by the multitude of thine iniquities, by the iniquity of thy traffick; therefore, will I bring forth a fire from the midst of thee, it shall devour thee, and I will bring thee to ashes upon the earth in the sight of all them that behold thee.

Eze 28:18

All they that know thee among the people shall be astonished at thee: thou shalt be a terror, and never shalt thou be anymore.

Eze 28:19

Thus, saith the Lord GOD; In the day when he went down to the grave I caused a mourning: I covered the deep for him, and I restrained the floods thereof, and the great waters were stayed: and I caused Lebanon to mourn for him, and all the trees of the field fainted for him.

Eze 31:15

I made the nations to shake at the sound of his fall when I cast him down to hell with them that descend into the pit: and all the trees of Eden, the choice and best of Lebanon, all that drink water, shall be comforted in the nether parts of the earth.

Eze 31:16

They also went down into hell with him unto them that be slain with the sword; and they that were his arm, that dwelt under his shadow in the midst of the heathen.

Eze 31:17

To whom art thou thus like in glory and in greatness among the trees of Eden? yet shalt thou be brought down with the trees of Eden unto the nether parts of the earth: thou shalt lie in the midst of the uncircumcised with them that be slain by the sword. This is Pharaoh and all his multitude, saith the Lord GOD.

Eze 31:18

As we learned his name is Lucifer. He allowed pride to enter his heart and wanted to be God. So, Lucifer tried to overthrow God. There was war in heaven. Revelation 12 tells us this,

And there appeared a great wonder in heaven; a woman clothed with the sun, and the moon under her feet, and upon her head a crown of twelve stars:

Rev 12:1

And she being with child cried, travailing in birth, and pained to be delivered.

Rev 12:2

And there appeared another wonder in heaven; and behold a great

red dragon, having seven heads and ten horns, and seven crowns upon his heads.

Rev 12:3

And his tail drew the third part of the stars of heaven, and did cast them to the earth: and the dragon stood before the woman which was ready to be delivered, for to devour her child as soon as it was born.

Rev 12:4

And she brought forth a man child, who was to rule all nations with a rod of iron: and her child was caught up unto God, and to his throne.

Rev 12:5

And the woman fled into the wilderness, where she hath a place prepared of God, that they should feed her there a thousand two hundred and threescore days.

Rev 12:6

And there was war in heaven: Michael and his angels fought against the dragon, and the dragon fought and his angels,

Rev 12:7

And prevailed not; neither was their place found anymore in heaven.

Rev 12:8

And the great dragon was cast out, that old serpent, called the Devil, and Satan, which deceiveth the whole world: he was cast out into the earth, and his angels were cast out with him.

Rev 12:9

And I heard a loud voice saying in heaven, Now is come salvation, and strength, and the kingdom of our God, and the power of his Christ: for the accuser of our brethren is cast down, which accused them before our God day and night.

Rev 12:10

And they overcame him by the blood of the Lamb, and by the word of their testimony, and they loved not their lives unto the death.

Rev 12:11

Therefore rejoice, ye heavens, and ye that dwell in them. Woe to the inhabiters of the earth and of the sea! for the devil is come down unto you, having great wrath, because he knoweth that he hath but a short time.

Rev 12:12

And when the dragon saw that he was cast unto the earth, he persecuted the woman which brought forth the man child.

Rev 12:13

And to the woman were given two wings of a great eagle, that she might fly into the wilderness, into her place, where she is nourished for a time and times, and half a time, from the face of the serpent.

Rev 12:14

And the serpent cast out of his mouth water as a flood after the woman, that he might cause her to be carried away of the flood.

Rev 12:15

And the earth helped the woman, and the earth opened her mouth, and swallowed up the flood which the dragon cast out of his mouth.

Rev 12:16

And the dragon was wroth with the woman and went to make war with the remnant of her seed, which keeps the commandments of God, and have the testimony of Jesus Christ.

Rev 12:17

Church, there is a war that is going on now, and this war will never end until the last judgment is given out.

From heaven, Lucifer was sent to earth. To earth, did he come up with a deceiving tactic on man? A man was created to worship God and to work in the Garden of Eden, but, as with all of God's creation, the serpent, also called Satan, wanted to be on top, so he deceived woman and man. Let us look at what the scriptures say that took place, Genesis 3,

Now the serpent was more subtil than any beast of the field which the LORD God had made. And he said unto the woman, Yea, hath God said, Ye shall not eat of every tree of the garden?

Gen 3:1

And the woman said unto the serpent, We may eat of the fruit of the trees of the garden:

Gen 3:2

But of the fruit of the tree which is in the midst of the garden, God hath said, Ye shall not eat of it, neither shall ye touch it, lest ye die.

Gen 3:3

And the serpent said unto the woman, Ye shall not surely die:

Gen 3:4

For God doth know that in the day ye eat thereof, then your eyes shall be opened, and ye shall be as gods, knowing good and evil.

Gen 3:5

And when the woman saw that the tree was good for food and that it was pleasant to the eyes, and a tree to be desired to make one wise, she took of the fruit thereof, and did eat, and gave also unto her husband with her; and he did eat.

Gen 3:6

And the eyes of them both were opened, and they knew that they were naked, and they sewed fig leaves together, and made themselves aprons.

Gen 3:7

And they heard the voice of the LORD God walking in the garden in the cool of the day: and Adam and his wife hid themselves from the presence of the LORD God amongst the trees of the garden.

Gen 3:8

And the LORD God called unto Adam, and said unto him, Where art thou?

Gen 3:9

And he said, I heard thy voice in the garden, and I was afraid, because I was naked; and I hid myself.

Gen 3:10

And he said, Who told thee that thou wast naked? Hast thou eaten of the tree, whereof I commanded thee that thou shouldest not eat?

Gen 3:11

And the man said, The woman whom thou gavest to be with me, she gave me of the tree, and I did eat.

Gen 3:12

And the LORD God said unto the woman, What is this that thou hast done? And the woman said, The serpent beguiled me, and I did eat.

Gen 3:13

And the LORD God said unto the serpent Because thou hast done this, thou art cursed above all cattle, and above every beast of the field; upon thy belly shalt thou go, and dust shalt thou eat all the days of thy life:

Gen 3:14

And I will put enmity between thee and the woman, and between thy seed and her seed; it shall bruise thy head, and thou shalt bruise his heel.

Gen 3:15

Unto the woman he said, I will greatly multiply thy sorrow and thy conception; in sorrow, thou shalt bring forth children; and thy desire shall be to thy husband, and he shall rule over thee.

Gen 3:16

And unto Adam, he said, Because thou hast hearkened unto the voice of thy wife, and hast eaten of the tree, of which I commanded thee, saying, Thou shalt not eat of it: cursed is the ground for thy sake; in sorrow shalt, thou eat of it all the days of thy life;

Gen 3:17

Thorns also and thistles shall it bring forth to thee; and thou shalt eat the herb of the field;

Gen 3:18

In the sweat of thy face shalt thou eat bread, till thou return unto the ground; for out of it wast thou taken: for dust thou art, and unto dust shalt thou return.

Gen 3:19

And Adam called his wife's name Eve; because she was the mother of all living.

Gen 3:20

Unto Adam also and to his wife did the LORD God make coats of skins, and clothed them.

Gen 3:21

And the LORD God said, Behold, the man is become as one of us, to know good and evil: and now, lest he put forth his hand, and take also of the tree of life, and eat, and live for ever:

Gen 3:22

Therefore, the LORD God sent him forth from the garden of Eden, to till the ground from whence he was taken.

Gen 3:23

So, he drove out the man, and he placed at the east of the garden of Eden Cherubims, and a flaming sword which turned every way, to keep the way of the tree of life.

Gen 3:24

So here we read about the fall of the man, and the war begins on our souls. Satan was a beautiful creation, but in his sin and his pride, he used the serpent, caused the serpent to crawl on his belly, and caused man and woman to be separated from God.

Satan goes before the throne of God, and he falsely accuses man of his wrongdoings, let us look at this:

Now there was a day when the sons of God came to present themselves before the LORD, and Satan came also among them.

Job 1:6

And the LORD said unto Satan, Whence comest thou? Then Satan answered the LORD, and said, From going to and fro in the earth, and from walking up and down in it.

Job 1:7

And the LORD said unto Satan, Hast thou considered my servant Job, that there is none like him in the earth, a perfect and an upright man, one that feareth God, and escheweth evil?

Job 1:8

Then Satan answered the LORD, and said, Doth Job fear God for nought?

Job 1:9

Hast not thou made a hedge about him, and about his house, and about all that he hath on every side? thou hast blessed the work of his hands, and his substance is increased in the land.

Job 1:10

But put forth thine hand now, and touch all that he hath, and he will curse thee to thy face.

Job 1:11

And the LORD said unto Satan, Behold, all that he hath is in thy power; only upon himself put not forth thine hand. So, Satan went forth from the presence of the LORD.

Job 1:12

And I heard a loud voice saying in heaven, Now is come salvation and strength, and the kingdom of our God, and the power of his Christ: for the accuser of our brethren is cast down, which accused them before our God day and night.

Rev 12:10

And they overcame him by the blood of the Lamb, and by the word of their testimony, and they loved not their lives unto the death.

Rev 12:11

Satan may falsely accuse us, but we have a higher power to attack him back. We are overcome by the blood of the lamb (Jesus Christ) and by the word of our testimony. We can defeat Satan through the blood of Jesus.

Satan has an end and he knows has an end, so he wants to take all he can with him to the lake of fire and be tormented for eternity. In the next verse, Revelation 12:13 tells us, "Therefore, rejoice, ye heavens, and ye that dwell in them. Woe to the inhabiters of the earth and of the sea! for the devil is come down unto you, having great wrath, because he knoweth that he hath but a short time."

Satan knows he has a short time, so he is working overtime, so he can take anyone with him to the lake of fire.

There is good news, there was a man, a God-man that came from heaven, that was sent from God, the Father, to forgive all sins and overcome the legion of Satan. Thus, we, the children of God, through the blood and resurrection of Jesus Christ.

But now is Christ risen from the dead, and become the first fruits of them that slept.

1Co 15:20

For since by man came death, by man came also the resurrection of the dead.

1Co 15:21

For as in Adam all die, even so in Christ shall all be made alive.

1Co 15:22

But every man in his own order: Christ the first fruits; afterward they that are Christ's at his coming.

1Co 15:23

You see, Adam fell in the beginning, as we learn, but Jesus became our victor. It is only through Jesus Christ we can attack our enemy.

So, what will be the end of Satan? Let us look at Revelation 20.

And I saw an angel come down from heaven, having the key of the bottomless pit and a great chain in his hand.

Rev 20:1

And he laid hold on the dragon, that old serpent, which is the Devil, and Satan, and bound him a thousand years,

Rev 20:2

And cast him into the bottomless pit, and shut him up, and set a seal upon him, that he should deceive the nations no more, till the thousand years should be fulfilled: and after that, he must be loosed a little season.

Rev 20:3

And I saw thrones, and they sat upon them, and judgment was given unto them: and I saw the souls of them that were beheaded for the witness of Jesus, and for the word of God, and which had not worshipped the beast, neither his image, neither had received his mark upon their foreheads, nor in their hands; and they lived and reigned with Christ a thousand years.

Rev 20:4

But the rest of the dead lived not again until the thousand years were finished. This is the first resurrection.

Rev 20:5

Blessed and holy is he that hath part in the first resurrection: on such the second death hath no power, but they shall be priests of God and of Christ and shall reign with him a thousand years.

Rev 20:6

And when the thousand years are expired, Satan shall be loosed out of his prison,

Rev 20:7

And shall go out to deceive the nations which are in the four quarters of the earth, Gog and Magog, to gather them together to battle: the number of whom is as the sand of the sea.

Rev 20:8

And they went up on the breadth of the earth, and compassed the camp of the saints about, and the beloved city: and fire came down from God out of heaven, and devoured them.

Rev 20:9

And the devil that deceived them was cast into the lake of fire and brimstone, where the beast and the false prophet are, and shall be tormented day and night forever and ever.

Rev 20:10

And I saw a great white throne, and him that sat on it, from whose face the earth and the heaven fled away; and there was found no place for them.

Rev 20:11

And I saw the dead, small and great, stand before God, and the books were opened: and another book was opened, which is the book of life: and the dead were judged out of those things which were written in the books, according to their works.

Rev 20:12

And the sea gave up the dead which were in it, and death and hell delivered up the dead which were in them: and they were judged every man according to their works.

Rev 20:13

And death and hell were cast into the lake of fire. This is the second death.

Rev 20:14

And whosoever was not found written in the book of life was cast into the lake of fire.

Rev 20:15

Here we read the end of Satan. He is cast into the bottomless pit, loosed for a season, and then he is overthrown by Christ and cast into the lake of fire along with death and hell.

Once again, St. Paul tells us we are not ignorant of Satan's tactics. It is in the word of God that we learn who our enemy is. In the word of God, we learn how to attack back Satan. Jesus was and is our perfect answer; looking at

Matthew4:1-11

Then was Jesus led up of the Spirit into the wilderness to be tempted of the devil.

Mat 4:1

And when he had fasted forty days and forty nights, he was afterward a hungered.

Mat 4:2

And when the tempter came to him, he said, If thou be the Son of God, command that these stones be made bread.

Mat 4:3

But he answered and said, It is written, Man shall not live by bread alone, but by every word that proceedeth out of the mouth of God.

Mat 4:4

Then the devil taketh him up into the holy city, and setteth him on a pinnacle of the temple,

Mat 4:5

And saith unto him, If thou be the Son of God, cast thyself down: for it is written, He shall give his angels charge concerning thee: and in their hands, they shall bear thee up, lest at any time thou dash thy foot against a stone.

Mat 4:6

Jesus said unto him, It is written again, Thou shalt not tempt the Lord thy God.

Mat 4:7

Again, the devil taketh him up into an exceeding high mountain, and sheweth him all the kingdoms of the world, and the glory of them;

Mat 4:8

And saith unto him, All these things will I give thee, if thou wilt fall down and worship me.

Mat 4:9

Then saith Jesus unto him, Get thee hence, Satan: for it is written, Thou shalt worship the Lord thy God, and him only shalt thou serve.

Mat 4:10

Then the devil leaveth him, and, behold, angels came and ministered unto him.

Mat 4:11

Jesus used the word of God to attack the devil after fasting forty days and nights looking at the eleventh verse, the angels came and ministered unto him. At the end of the temptation, Jesus obtained a greater blessing.

We may go through manifold temptations, but if we stay true to God and attack with his word, then we will overcome.

I can do all things through Christ which strengtheneth me.

Philippians 4:12

Chapter 3 Attack on Lust

Lust. Once again, let us look at Webster's dictionary for the meaning of this word.

Definition 1. excessive sexual desire 2. overmastering desire, such as lust for power.

Lust can be more than a sexual desire; it can be after any sin. So, what do the scriptures tell us about lust? In the book of James, chapter 1 verses 12 through verse 16 tell you what lust can do.

Blessed is the man that endureth temptation: for when he is tried, he shall receive the crown of life, which the Lord hath promised to them that love him.

James 1:12

Let no man say when he is tempted, I am tempted of God: for God cannot be tempted with evil, neither tempteth he any man:

James 1:13

But every man is tempted, when he is drawn away of his own lust, and enticed.

James 1:14

Then when lust hath conceived, it bringeth forth sin: and sin, when it is finished, bringeth forth death.

James 1:15

Do not err, my beloved brethren.

James 1:16

Notice there are three parts to these scriptures, called spiritual L.S.D. (lust, sin, death). An addiction has a beginning like an alcoholic begins with one drink. So, as with lust, it has a beginning, but we, as Christians, can attack this from the start. The beginning is called Temptation. The temptation may be a love of money, power, sex, drugs, and the list goes on and on. When we see a temptation come our way and we endure that trial of faith, we can attack the temptation with prayer and Bible study. Then we shall overcome and obtain the crown of life when we endure to the end.

If we fall into temptation, then it becomes lust; after lust, it turns into sin and then sin causes death. This is a spiritual death. Notice what James says in chapter one, verse sixteen, *"Do not err, my beloved brethren."*

James is speaking to the Christian, not to the sinner. So, yes, you can weaken and see the death of your own soul.

So, how do we attack L.S.D.? By abiding in the vine. Jesus said this in the book of John 15:1-8,

I am the true vine, and my Father is the husbandman.

Joh 15:1

Every branch in me that beareth not fruit he taketh away: and every branch that beareth fruit, he purgeth it, that it may bring forth more fruit.

Joh 15:2

Now ye are clean through the word which I have spoken unto you.

Joh 15:3

Abide in me, and I in you. As the branch cannot bear fruit of itself, except it abide in the vine; no more can ye, except ye abide in me.

Joh 15:4

I am the vine, ye are the branches: He that abideth in me, and I in him, the same bringeth forth much fruit: for without me ye can do nothing.

Joh 15:5

If a man abide not in me, he is cast forth as a branch, and is withered; and men gather them, and cast them into the fire, and they are burned.

Joh 15:6

If ye abide in me, and my words abide in you, ye shall ask what ye will, and it shall be done unto you.

Joh 15:7

Herein is my Father glorified, that ye bear much fruit; so shall ye be my disciples.

Joh 15:8

We must abide in the vine to stay alive and yield good fruit. How do you yield yourself? Romans tells us this,

Know ye not, that to whom ye yield yourselves servants to obey, his servants ye are to whom ye obey; whether of sin unto death, or of obedience unto righteousness?

Rom 6:16

But God be thanked, that ye were the servants of sin, but ye have obeyed from the heart that form of doctrine which was delivered you.

Rom 6:17

Being then made free from sin, ye became the servants of righteousness.

Rom 6:18

I speak after the manner of men because of the infirmity of your flesh: for as ye have yielded your member's servants to uncleanness and to iniquity unto iniquity; even so now yield your member's servants to righteousness unto holiness.

Rom 6:19

For when ye were the servants of sin, ye were free from righteousness.

Rom 6:20

What fruit had ye then in those things whereof ye are now ashamed? for the end of those things is death.

Rom 6:21

But now being made free from sin, and become servants to God, ye have your fruit unto holiness, and the end everlasting life.

Rom 6:22

For the wages of sin is death, but the gift of God is eternal life through Jesus Christ our Lord.

Rom 6:23

Looking at what the scriptures say, we read that if we yield ourselves and be obedient unto righteousness, we shall be an over-comer. When we overcome, we get the ability to attack.

When we were still sinners we were a servant unto sin and not a servant unto the Lord Jesus.

When we get saved we are saved from our sins, not in our sins,

Romans 6:1-2

What shall we say then? Shall we continue in sin, that grace may abound?

Rom 6:1

God forbid. How shall we, that are dead to sin, live any longer therein?

Rom 6:2

When we get saved, we also repent, thus meaning to turn away from sin. We begin to abide in the vine. Is it a sin to be tempted? No! Let us look in the book of Hebrews,

Seeing then that we have a great high priest, that is passed into the heavens, Jesus, the Son of God, let us hold fast our profession.

Heb 4:14

For we have not a high priest which cannot be touched with the feeling of our infirmities; but was in all points tempted like as we are, yet without sin.

Heb 4:15

Let us therefore come boldly unto the throne of grace, that we may obtain mercy, and find grace to help in time of need.

Heb 4:16

Jesus was tempted to all points as we are tempted yet without sin. So being tempted is not a sin.

At this time, let us look at seven temptations and seven sins in the book of

Proverbs 6:16-19.

These six things doth the LORD hate: yea, seven are an abomination unto him:

Pro 6:16

A proud look, a lying tongue, and hands that shed innocent blood,

Pro 6:17

A heart that deviseth wicked imaginations, feet that be swift in running to mischief,

Pro 6:18

A false witness that speaketh lies, and he that soweth discord among brethren

Pro 6:19

These seven sins are also seven temptations. Whether we like it or not, we all have done one of these sins at one time or the other. What about if we commit sin after we are saved? Is there forgiveness? Yes, there is, John tells us this,

My little children, these things write I unto you, that ye sin not. And if any man sins, we have an advocate with the Father, Jesus Christ the righteous:

1John 2:1

And he is the propitiation for our sins: and not for ours only, but also for the sins of the whole world.

1John 2:2

And hereby we do know that we know him if we keep his commandments.

1John 2:3

Yes, there is forgiveness, but it's best to keep his commandments and walk holy before the Lord. And love his word.

By yielding ourselves unto Jesus Christ and using ourselves for the glory of the cross of Christ, we will come under the grace of Jesus and the mercy of God our Father.

How do we resist temptation and the lust of the flesh? Pray, pray, pray. By praying to the Lord, we can attack and overcome lust at its core.

Chapter 4 Attack on Witchcraft

The church is in a spiritual warfare, a fight for the soul of man. God has his pastors, prophets, teachers, and singers. Satan also has agents; they are false prophets, warlocks, witches, and soothsayers.

What does God say about these? Let us look more into the scriptures for the meaning.

When thou art come into the land which the LORD thy God giveth thee, thou shalt not learn to do after the abominations of those nations.

Deut 18:9

There shall not be found among you anyone that maketh his son or his daughter to pass through the fire, or that useth divination, or an observer of times, or an enchanter, or a witch,

Deut 18:10

Or a charmer, or a consulter with familiar spirits, or a wizard, or a necromancer.

Deut 18:11

For all that do these things are an abomination unto the LORD: and because of these abominations the LORD thy God doth drive them out from before thee.

Deut 18:12

Thou shalt be perfect with the LORD thy God.

Deut 18:13

For these nations, which thou shalt possess, hearkened unto observers of times, and unto diviners: but as for thee, the LORD thy God hath not suffered thee so to do.

Deut 18:14

God warns his people against child sacrifice; this practice was done unto a pagan god called Moloch,

And thou shalt not let any of thy seed pass through the fire to Molech, neither shalt thou profane the name of thy God: I am the LORD.

Lev 18:21

Molech or Moloch was an Ammo-nite god in; when they worshiped this god, they would have gruesome orgies and a child sacrifice. At times the god-like figure was heated by fire, and the child was placed in the arms of Moloch, and the child burned alive.

Today the practice of child sacrifice continues right on. Thousands of babies are killed every day by abortion. They (the government) will try and tell you that it is a woman's right to have an abortion. It is no one's right to take a life from a mother's womb. Life begins at the time of conception, and a soul is given to that baby from the giver of life, God the Father.

I like to express more on this subject and bring out a double standard between the government and the laws that are in the land. A woman and an unborn child are murdered by another person, and this person goes to trial and gets charged with not a single but a double murder. But, let an abortion take place, and there is no murder. At least, that is what the law says. Either way, both are murders. Yes, abortion is a sin of witchcraft. How are we to attack this sin? We are to sanctify ourselves or to set ourselves apart from this worldly practice.

Divination, what does this mean? The means of foretelling the future by occult ways. We see this all over; it is in the newspaper called the horoscope, on T.V., on the Internet, and on the phone. Astrologers are trying to tell you your future for so much money, and they will predict it. Then we have so-called prophets telling you to sow money in their ministries, and they will prophesy over your smooth things while all the time they are serving the prince of this world.

We as Christians, need to be holy unto God, we need to set ourselves apart from this sin called divination. Let us look at

Leviticus 11:44-45 and in 1 Peter 11:13-14,

For I am the LORD your God: ye shall therefore sanctify yourselves, and ye shall be holy; for I am holy: neither shall ye defile yourselves

with any manner of creeping thing that creepeth upon the earth.

Lev 11:44

For I am the LORD that bringeth you up out of the land of Egypt, to be your God: ye shall therefore be holy, for I am holy.

Lev 11:45

As obedient children, not fashioning yourselves according to the former lusts in your ignorance:

1Pe 1:14

But as he which hath called you is holy, so be ye holy in all manner of conversation;

1Pe 1:15

Because it is written, Be ye holy; for I am holy.

1Pe 1:16

We serve a holy God. There is but one God; he is the Father. God sent his only son Jesus Christ (John 3:16), to die for our sins. God manifested himself through Jesus Christ. Jesus represented the Father through himself, thus becoming one with the Father (John 10:30). Jesus has given us the authority to be one with himself and the Father,

John 17:15-21.

I pray not that thou shouldest take them out of the world, but that thou shouldest keep them from the evil.

John 17:15

They are not of the world, even as I am not of the world.

John 17:16

Sanctify them through thy truth: thy word is truth.

John 17:17

As thou hast sent me into the world, even so have I also sent them into the world.

John 17:18

And for their sakes I sanctify myself, that they also might be sanctified through the truth.

John 17:19

Neither pray I for these alone, but for them also which shall believe on me through their word;

John 17:20

That they all may be one; as thou, Father, art in me, and I in thee, that they also may be one in us: that the world may believe that thou hast sent me

John 17:21

So, by us becoming one with Jesus Christ, we sanctify ourselves from the world. Does this mean we are equal to God? No, we are not. We become one the Father through Jesus Christ. We are sanctified through the blood of Jesus.

We, as Christians, need to be holy unto God. We need to set ourselves apart from this sin called divination.

We serve a holy God, so, therefore, we are to be holy. By being holy, we attack these sins. Let us continue on looking at more of these sins.

Observer of times. What do they do? An observer of times is a person who practices magic potions and performs spells. We can see this in the book of Daniel. Daniel and his three friends kept themselves holy unto the Lord, and God blessed them and kept them in favor with all the kings of Babylon. Just as these men did, we can attack the enemy by living right(holy) unto the Lord.

A witch is an evil entity. A good or bad witch doesn't exist, they all are evil, and their master is Satan. The end of a witch is hell.

A charmer is a person who charms you into doing things that are evil. The charmer will make it look so enticing and fun, but their agenda is death; their goal is pure evil.

We have seen on these talk shows to have a consulter to talk to your loved ones who are dead. Or you may hear of someone performing séance at your house to call up a dead loved one to speak to you or to give you advice. This act is also called a consulter. This is a sin to the very core.

A wizard is a male witch. Hollywood has glamorized witches and wizards to no end. But the truth is that demons control their soul, and if they do not repent, then in hell and the lake of fire they will burn with their master called Lucifer or Satan.

A Necromancer, what does this person do? This person deals directly with a dead body. In many cases, a necromancer will sleep with a dead body. Jesus told us this in Matt 8:22 to let the dead bury the dead.

In closing with this chapter, I want to look at King Saul and see what happened to him by dealing with witchcraft.

1 Samuel 28:3-25

Now Samuel was dead, and all Israel had lamented him, and buried him in Ramah, even in his own city. And Saul had put away those that had familiar spirits, and the wizards, out of the land.

1Sa 28:3

And the Philistines gathered themselves together, and came and pitched in Shunem: and Saul gathered all Israel together, and they pitched in Gilboa.

1Sa 28:4

And when Saul saw the host of the Philistines, he was afraid, and his heart greatly trembled.

1Sa 28:5

And when Saul enquired of the LORD, the LORD answered him not, neither by dreams, nor by Urim, nor by prophets.

1Sa 28:6

Then said Saul unto his servants, Seek me a woman that hath a familiar spirit, that I may go to her, and enquire of her. And his servants said to him, Behold, there is a woman that hath a familiar spirit at Endor.

1Sa 28:7

And Saul disguised himself, and put on other raiments, and he went, and two men with him, and they came to the woman by night: and he said, I pray thee, divine unto me by the familiar spirit, and bring me him up, whom I shall name unto thee.

1Sa 28:8

And the woman said unto him, Behold, thou knowest what Saul hath done, how he hath cut off those that have familiar spirits, and the wizards, out of the land: wherefore then layest thou a snare for my life, to cause me to die?

1Sa 28:9

And Saul sware to her by the LORD, saying, As the LORD liveth, there shall no punishment happen to thee for this thing.

1Sa 28:10

Then said the woman, Whom shall I bring up unto thee? And he said, Bring me up, Samuel.

1Sa 28:11

And when the woman saw Samuel, she cried with a loud voice: and the woman spake to Saul, saying, Why hast thou deceived me? for thou art Saul.

1Sa 28:12

And the king said unto her, Be not afraid: for what sawest thou? And the woman said unto Saul, I saw gods ascending out of the earth.

1Sa 28:13

And he said unto her, What form is he of? And she said, An old man cometh up, and he is covered with a mantle. And Saul perceived that it was Samuel, and he stooped with his face to the ground and bowed himself.

1Sa 28:14

And Samuel said to Saul, Why hast thou disquieted me, to bring me up? And Saul answered I am sore distressed; for the Philistines make war against me, and God is departed from me, and answereth me no more, neither by prophets nor by dreams: therefore, I have called thee, that thou mayest make known unto me what I shall do.

1Sa 28:15

Then said Samuel, Wherefore then dost thou ask of me, seeing the LORD is departed from thee, and is become thine enemy?

1Sa 28:16

And the LORD hath done to him, as he spake by me: for the LORD hath rent the kingdom out of thine hand, and given it to thy neighbour, even to David:

1Sa 28:17

Because thou obeyedst not the voice of the LORD, nor executedst his fierce wrath upon Amalek, therefore hath the LORD done this thing unto thee this day.

1Sa 28:18

Moreover, the LORD will also deliver Israel with thee into the hand of the Philistines: and tomorrow shalt thou and thy sons be with me: the LORD also shall deliver the host of Israel into the hand of the Philistines.

1Sa 28:19

Then Saul fell straightway all along on the earth, and was sore afraid, because of the words of Samuel: and there was no strength in him; for he had eaten no bread all the day, nor all the night.

1Sa 28:20

And the woman came unto Saul, and saw that he was sore troubled, and said unto him, Behold, thine handmaid hath obeyed thy voice, and I have put my life in my hand, and have hearkened unto thy words which thou spakest unto me.

1Sa 28:21

Now therefore, I pray thee, hearken thou also unto the voice of thine handmaid, and let me set a morsel of bread before thee; and eat, that thou mayest have strength when thou goest on thy way.

1Sa 28:22

But he refused, and said, I will not eat. But his servants, together with the woman, compelled him; and he hearkened unto their voice. So, he arose from the earth and sat upon the bed.

1Sa 28:23

And the woman had a fat calf in the house, and she hasted, and killed it, and took flour, and kneaded it, and did bake unleavened bread thereof:

1Sa 28:24

And she brought it before Saul, and before his servants; and they did eat. Then they rose up and went away that night.

1Sa 28:25

King Saul went to the lowest of the low. It is sad, but many Christians have forsaken the cross and gone to an all-time low.

The church, we are well able to attack these evil spirits by prayer and fasting through the cross of Christ.

Chapter 5 Attack on Gossip

Gossip. What, a subject to attack. Regardless of who you are or what you have done, we all have gossip at one time or the other.

Webster's dictionary tells us the meaning of the word gossip. 1. One who chatters idly or repeats rumors about others.

The tongue is one of the smallest members of the body but, it is also the sharpest member of the body. James 3:5-12 tells us this,

Even so, the tongue is a little member, and boasteth great things. Behold, how great a matter a little fire kindleth!

Jas 3:5

And the tongue is a fire, a world of iniquity: so is the tongue among our members, that it defileth the whole body, and setteth on fire the course of nature; and it is set on fire of hell.

Jas 3:6

For every kind of beasts, and of birds, and of serpents, and of things in the sea, is tamed, and hath been tamed of mankind:

Jas 3:7

But the tongue can no man tame; it is an unruly evil, full of deadly poison.

Jas 3:8

Therewith bless we, God, even the Father; and therewith curse we men, which are made after the similitude of God.

Jas 3:9

Out of the same mouth proceedeth blessing and cursing. My brethren, these things ought not so to be.

Jas 3:10

Doth a fountain send forth at the same place sweet water and bitter?

Jas 3:11

Can the fig tree, my brethren, bear olive berries? either a vine or figs? so can no fountain both yield salt water and fresh?

Jas 3:12

Can the tongue be tamed? No! A man cannot tame the tongue. The tongue can speak a curse or speak a blessing. Genesis 9: 18-29 tells us how Noah cursed Canaan and blessed Shem.

And the sons of Noah, that went forth of the ark, were Shem, and Ham, and Japheth: and Ham is the father of Canaan.

Gen 9:18

These are the three sons of Noah: and of them was the whole earth overspread.

Gen 9:19

And Noah began to be a husbandman, and he planted a vineyard:

Gen 9:20

And he drank of the wine, and was drunken, and he was uncovered within his tent.

Gen 9:21

And Ham, the father of Canaan, saw the nakedness of his father and told his two brethren without.

Gen 9:22

And Shem and Japheth took a garment, and laid it upon both their shoulders, and went backward, and covered the nakedness of their father, and their faces were backward, and they saw not their father's nakedness.

Gen 9:23

And Noah awoke from his wine and knew what his younger son had done unto him.

Gen 9:24

And he said, Cursed be Canaan; a servant of servants shall he be unto his brethren.

Gen 9:25

And he said, Blessed be the LORD God of Shem, and Canaan shall be his servant.

Gen 9:26

God shall enlarge Japheth, and he shall dwell in the tents of Shem, and Canaan shall be his servant.

Gen 9:27

And Noah lived after the flood three hundred and fifty years.

Gen 9:28

And all the days of Noah were nine hundred and fifty years: and he died.

Gen 9:29

A curse is speaking against that person, and a Blessing is speaking good tidings unto that person.

The church never ceases to amaze me. When you think you have seen it all, something new will always arise, some good and some bad. I am forty-three at the writing of this book, and I have been preaching for 30 years, and I have seen this in church people. They go to church and speak blessings, but no sooner than when they get in the car to go home are they ready to condemn the same people they were in church with.

A double-minded man is unstable in all his ways.

James 1:8

A person can use their tongue to start rumours and lies, which is called gossip or a lie. James tells us this; these things ought not to be. We as Christians must speak the same as in church; we are not to be unstable in our words.

When we speak blessings on people around us, we will receive blessings.

We speak cursing on people around us, then cursing will we receive.

Cast thy bread upon the waters: for thou shalt find it after many days.

Ecc 11:1

Be not deceived; God is not mocked: for whatsoever a man soweth, that shall he also reap.

Gal 6:7

For he that soweth to his flesh shall of the flesh reap corruption; but he that soweth to the Spirit shall of the Spirit reap life everlasting.

Gal 6:8

And let us not be weary in well doing: for in due season we shall reap if we faint not.

Gal 6:9

As we have therefore opportunity, let us do good unto all men, especially unto them who are of the household of faith.

Gal 6:10

Whatever we sow we shall reap. James 3:13 tells us this, Who is a wise man and endued with knowledge among you? let him shew out of a good conversation his works with meekness of wisdom.

Jas 3:13

Wisdom comes from above; knowledge is knowing to do good or evil. It is when we use the knowledge for good it becomes wisdom, but all wisdom comes from above.

Gossip, cursing, and bad language (cussing) will cause strife.

This is a sin.

Words have power; the sooner we learn this, the better off we will be. At this time, I want to look at the book of

Proverbs 12:15- 23,

The way of a fool is right in his own eyes: but he that hearkeneth unto counsel is wise.

Pro 12:15

A fool's wrath is presently known: but a prudent man covereth shame.

Pro 12:16

He that speaketh truth sheweth forth righteousness: but false witness deceit.

Pro 12:17

There is that speaketh like the piercings of a sword: but the tongue of the wise is health.

Pro 12:18

The lip of truth shall be established forever: but a lying tongue is but for a moment.

Pro 12:19

Deceit is in the heart of them that imagine evil: but to the counsellors of peace is joy.

Pro 12:20

There shall no evil happen to the just: but the wicked shall be filled with mischief.

Pro 12:21

Lying lips are an abomination to the LORD: but they that deal truly are his delight.

Pro 12:22

A prudent man concealeth knowledge: but the heart of fools proclaimeth foolishness.

Pro 12:23

I believe the scriptures speak for themselves. Words will help or be harmful.

My dad has always told me, Sam, there is a time to speak, and there is a time to be quiet. Solomon said it best in

Eccl 3:1-8,

To everything there is a season, and a time to every purpose under

the heaven:

Ecc 3:1

A time to be born, and a time to die; a time to plant, and a time to pluck up that which is planted;

Ecc 3:2

A time to kill, and a time to heal; a time to break down, and a time to build up;

Ecc 3:3

A time to weep, and a time to laugh; a time to mourn, and a time to dance;

Ecc 3:4

A time to cast away stones, and a time to gather stones together; a time to embrace, and a time to refrain from embracing;

Ecc 3:5

A time to get, and a time to lose; a time to keep, and a time to cast away;

Ecc 3:6

A time to rend, and a time to sew; a time to keep silence and a time to speak;

Ecc 3:7

A time to love, and a time to hate; a time of war, and a time of peace.

Ecc 3:8

There have been many people who have a good testimony and a good witness but by the time it is over, they tear down their own witness by the words they say and use. Let us learn to speak and to listen.

We can attack gossip by the words we use to speak. We allow the Holy Ghost to speak for us. Pray, pray, and pray to overcome.

Chapter 6 Attack on Excuse

The Pastor is about to walk out of the door for Sunday evening church and the phone rings. The Pastor's wife answers the phone. The pastor hears the conversation that is being said.

Let us listen, to this conversation that is being said on the phone.

The Phone rings, Sister Pastor answers the Phone, "Hi there, Sister Pastor this is Sister Somebody. Me and my husband cannot make it tonight. My husband has a slight fever and I have a slight cough. Can you pray for us? So please excuse us for not coming to church tonight."

Sister Pastor says, "Yes Sister Somebody, we will request

prayer for you and Brother Somebody." The phone clicks and they both hang up.

The wife says to her husband, "Honey, what are we going to do? So many are skipping church for simple excuses. I am so

worried about Brother and Sister Somebody. You know this makes the fifth service they have missed. They just make one excuse after another."

The Pastor looks at his wife and says, "Honey, all we can do is pray for Brother and Sister Somebody. Will you call them up and ask them for dinner and we will show them that we care for them and maybe we can encourage them."

This is just a small story. In all reality, this has happened to me and my wife. It has not happened to just us, but, it has happened to every Pastor and his wife.

My wife plays the piano and sings but, many pastors depend on others to play music, and when one is missing from the band they are missed very much.

The theme of this chapter is attacking excuses. There are many definitions of the word excuse: to be free from being at a certain place or to be excused from the dinner table.There is one appointment that a person will not be excused from.

In Hebrews 9:27-28,

And as it is appointed unto men once to die, but after this the judgment:

Heb 9:27

So, Christ was once offered to bear the sins of many; and unto them that look for him shall he appear the second time without sin unto salvation.

Heb 9:28

It is appointed for all flesh of man to die. Adam and Eve did that unto us when they fell in the Garden in the book of Genesis.

So how do we attack excuses? We must have a made-up mind. I have seen people come and they would be sick and by the time church service was over, they had received their healing and the Lord had moved on their behalf.

Today, People want to make an excuse not to come to church. We go to worship the Lord and lift his name on high, in return, God blesses his people.

So, is it a sin for a Christian to miss church? Let us examine what the scripture says. Hebrews 10:19-25 tells us this,

Having therefore, brethren, boldness to enter into the holiest by the blood of Jesus,

Heb 10:19

By a new and living way, which he hath consecrated for us, through the veil, that is to say, his flesh;

Heb 10:20

And having a high priest over the house of God;

Heb 10:21

Let us draw near with a true heart in full assurance of faith, having our hearts sprinkled from an evil conscience, and our bodies washed

with pure water.

Heb 10:22

Let us hold fast to the profession of our faith without wavering; (for he is faithful that promised;)

Heb 10:23

And let us consider one another to provoke unto love and to good works:

Heb 10:24

Not forsaking the assembling of ourselves together, as the manner of some is; but exhorting one another: and so much the more, as ye see the day approaching.

Heb 10:25

The high priest of the law could go only once a year into the holiest place on earth, but by the blood of Jesus Christ, the least of saints can have daily access to the holiest place in heaven.

The veil was rented from top to bottom.

And, behold, the veil of the temple was rent in twain from the top to the bottom; and the earth did quake, and the rocks rent;

Matt 27:51

Jesus made a way so we can have a way to the holiest. Jesus shed his blood for the atonement for our sins.

When a building is built for a church house, it is dedicated to being holy ground, thus making the place a holy place to gather and worship God. It takes people to come together to have church looking at verse 25; we are not to forsake the assembling together.

I feel that if you are with a body of believers, then when they set their services to have a church, then be faithful to the house of God. It takes people to have church. The church is from people, not from the building.

We must have boldness to enter into the holiest and that boldness belongs in the blood of Jesus Christ. In Jesus, there is a new and living way; this way is called salvation, thus making Jesus Christ our high priest.

As a church, we need to draw closer to the Lord with a true and faithful heart.

Let us profess our faith in Jesus and in Jesus alone. Having a love of God to encourage one another to do good. By coming together and not forsaking ourselves together, we will find the strength to go on and live right. So, is it a sin not to come to church? Yes, it can be a sin. When you feel that church does you no good, it is likely, that you have backslid, and you need to repent and get your eyes off of people and get your eyes on Jesus Christ.

There are numbers, without count, beyond excuses that people have made to keep from going to church.

Let us explore some of these excuses that Satan has put forth as truths, but, as we will find out from the scriptures, they are all lies. John 8:44 tells us this

Ye are of your father the devil, and the lusts of your father ye will do. He was a murderer from the beginning, and abode not in the truth because there is no truth in him. When he speaketh a lie, he speaketh of his own: for he is a liar and the father of it.

We learn that Satan is a murderer and the father of lies. With that being said, let us look at some of the excuses.

Let us look at six different excuses that are most common that people use.

Excuse one, "I am not a sinner." What a lie from the pits of hell. Looking into the scriptures, we will find that all have sinned.

But now the righteousness of God without the law is manifested, being witnessed by the law and the prophets;

Rom 3:21

Even the righteousness of God which is by faith of Jesus Christ unto all and upon all them that believe: for there is no difference:

Rom 3:22

For all have sinned, and come short of the glory of God;

Rom 3:23

Being justified freely by his grace through the redemption that is in Christ Jesus:

Rom 3:24

Whom God hath set forth to be a propitiation through faith in his blood, to declare his righteousness for the remission of sins that are past, through the forbearance of God;

Rom 3:25

To declare, I say, at this time his righteousness: that he might be just, and the justifier of him which believeth in Jesus.

Rom 3:26

We all have sinned; we all inherited sin from the fall of Adam and Eve.

When Adam and Eve disobeyed God and ate the fruit, sin became ingrained in them. Sin became part of man's DNA. Sin is what kills the body of flesh, but the soul can be reconciled back to the Father through Jesus Christ.

Therefore, if any man be in Christ, he is a new creature: old things are passed away; behold, all things are become new.

2Co 5:17

And all things are of God, who hath reconciled us to himself by Jesus Christ, and hath given to us the ministry of reconciliation;

2Co 5:18

To wit, that God was in Christ, reconciling the world unto himself, not imputing their trespasses unto them; and hath committed unto us the word of reconciliation.

2Co 5:19

It is only through Jesus that we can obtain our reconciliation.

Excuse 2, "I am too big of a sinner." As a minister, I have heard this lie repeated in my ears, way too many times. As a minister, I like to say this, Jesus came to save all sinners that call upon his name, not just a few people but to all.

And Jesus entered and passed through Jericho.

Luk 19:1

And, behold, there was a man named Zacchaeus, who was the chief among the publicans, and he was rich.

Luk 19:2

And he sought to see Jesus who he was; and could not for the press, because he was little of stature

Luk 19:3.

And he ran before and climbed up into a sycomore tree to see him: for he was to pass that way.

Luk 19:4

And when Jesus came to the place, he looked up, and saw him, and said unto him, Zacchaeus, make haste, and come down; for today I must abide at thy house.

Luk 19:5

And he made haste and came down, and received him joyfully.

Luk 19:6

And when they saw it, they all murmured, saying, That he was gone to be a guest with a man that is a sinner.

Luk 19:7

And Zacchaeus stood, and said unto the Lord; Behold, Lord, the half of my goods I give to the poor; and if I have taken anything from any man by false accusation, I restore him fourfold

Luk 19:8

And Jesus said unto him, This day is salvation come to this house, for so much as he also is a son of Abraham.

Luk 19:9

For the Son of man is come to seek and to save that which was lost.

Luk 19:10

A tax collector was called a publican; according to the Jews, a publican was called a sinner. Notice what Jesus said; he came to seek and to save that which was lost. WOW! We all have sinned; no matter if you lied, cheated, stole, killed, were a drunkard, or a druggie, no matter what you have done, you can be saved.

John 3:16-21,

For God so loved the world, that he gave his only begotten Son, that whosoever believeth in him should not perish, but have everlasting life.

John 3:16

For God sent not his Son into the world to condemn the world; but that the world through him might be saved.

John 3:17

He that believeth on him is not condemned: but he that believeth not is condemned already, because he hath not believed in the name of the only begotten Son of God.

John 3:18

And this is the condemnation, that light is come into the world, and men loved darkness rather than light because their deeds were evil.

John 3:19

For everyone that doeth evil hateth the light, neither cometh to the light, lest his deeds should be reproved.

John 3:20

But he that doeth truth cometh to the light, that his deeds may be made manifest, that they are wrought in God

John 3:21.

In Jesus Christ we become a new creation there is no more condemnation.

For when we were yet without strength, in due time Christ died for the ungodly.

Rom 5:6

For scarcely for a righteous man will one die: yet peradventure for a good man some would even dare to die.

Rom 5:7

But God commendeth his love toward us, in that, while we were yet sinners, Christ died for us.

Rom 5:8

Awesome! In due time, Jesus was in the beginning and saw us in our sins.

While we were yet sinners, Jesus died for our sins. This includes every person.

Looking at excuse three, "There are too many hypocrites in that church." if I had a dollar every time I heard this excuse, I would be a millionaire by now.

I will not dwell much on this. There is a chapter alone on this subject. Are there hypocrites in churches? Yes, they are. But we need not let a hypocrite steal our joy.

Excuse four, "My friends mean so much to me." If you allow a friend to keep you from getting saved, then they are not your friend. James 4:4 tells us this,

Ye adulterers and adulteresses, know ye not that the friendship of the world is enmity with God? whosoever therefore will be a friend of the world is the enemy of God.

Jas 4:4

The world is not your friend; the world of sin will take your soul to hell. Sin has a price to pay. The sting of death is sin, but the gift of God is eternal life.

Excuse five, "I am religious." If religion is all you have, then in hell, you will lift your eyes. Matthew 7:21- 23 tells us this,

Not everyone that saith unto me, Lord, Lord, shall enter into the kingdom of heaven; but he that doeth the will of my Father which is in heaven.

Mat 7:21

Many will say to me in that day, Lord, Lord, have we not prophesied in thy name? and in thy name have cast out devils? and in thy name done many wonderful works?

Mat 7:22

And then will I profess unto them, I never knew you: depart from me, ye that work iniquity.

Mat 7:23

Jesus spoke this very plainly, just because you believe, visit church on Easter and on Christmas services, or go to gospel singing does not make you a Christian. You must be born again.

Excuse six, "I intend to get saved before I die." What a lie from the pits of hell.

Seek ye the LORD while he may be found, call ye upon him while he is near:

Isa 55:6

Let the wicked forsake his way, and the unrighteous man his thoughts: and let him return unto the LORD, and he will have mercy upon him; and to our God, for he will abundantly pardon.

Isa 55:7

When God is near, when the Holy Ghost is dealing with your heart, that is the time to pray. Some of you may be reading this now, and God is dealing with your heart now. Now is the time to pray while God is near. James 4:13-17 tells this,

Go to now, ye that say, Today or tomorrow we will go into such a city, and continue there a year, and buy and sell, and get gain:

Jas 4:13

Whereas ye know not what shall be on the morrow. For what is your life? It is even a vapour, that appeareth for a little time, and then vanisheth away.

Jas 4:14

For that ye ought to say, If the Lord will, we shall live, and do this, or that.

Jas 4:15

But now ye rejoice in your boastings: all such rejoicing is evil.

Jas 4:16

Therefore, to him that knoweth to do good, and doeth it not, to him it is sin.

Jas 4:17

We have no guarantee for tomorrow except by the mercies of God. You may be in the street and be run over; you have a heart attack, no warning at all, and fall over dead. We have no assurance of tomorrow but by the grace of God.

I have explained just a few excuses that we need to attack in our lives. How do we attack these? By being faithful to Jesus Christ and his word. Let us attack by being on the firing line.

Chapter 7 Attack on Confusion

Confusion means to be in uncertainty. Let us look at a man who caused confusion in the church and for Paul. Let us read in Acts 19:21-41.

After these things were ended, Paul purposed in the spirit, when he had passed through Macedonia and Achaia, to go to Jerusalem, saying, After I have been there, I must also see Rome.

Act 19:21

S,o he sent into Macedonia two of them that ministered unto him, Timotheus and Erastus; but he himself stayed in Asia for a season.

Act 19:22

And the same time there arose no small stir about that way.

Act 19:23

For a certain man named Demetrius, a silversmith, which made silver shrines for Diana, brought no small gain unto the craftsmen;

Act 19:24

Whom he called together with the workmen of like occupation, and said, Sirs, ye know that by this craft we have our wealth.

Act 19:25

Moreover, ye see and hear, that not alone at Ephesus, but almost throughout all Asia, this Paul hath persuaded and turned away much people, saying that they be no gods, which are made with hands:

Act 19:26

So that not only this our craft is in danger to be set at nought; but also that the temple of the great goddess Diana should be despised, and her magnificence should be destroyed, whom all Asia and the world worshippeth.

Act 19:27

And when they heard these sayings, they were full of wrath, and cried out, saying, Great is Diana of the Ephesians.

Act 19:28

And the whole city was filled with confusion: and having caught Gaius and Aristarchus, men of Macedonia, Paul's companions in travel, they rushed with one accord into the theatre.

Act 19:29

And when Paul would have entered in unto the people, the disciples suffered him not.

Act 19:30

And certain of the chief of Asia, which were his friends, sent unto him, desiring him that he would not adventure himself into the theatre.

Act 19:31

Some, therefore, cried one thing, and some another: for the assembly was confused, and the more part knew not wherefore they were come together.

Act 19:32

And they drew Alexander out of the multitude, the Jews putting him forward. And Alexander beckoned with the hand and would have made his defence unto the people.

Act 19:33

But when they knew that he was a Jew, all with one voice about the space of two hours cried out, Great is Diana of the Ephesians.

Act 19:34

And when the town clerk had appeased the people, he said, Ye men of Ephesus, what man is there that knoweth not how that the city of the Ephesians is a worshipper of the great goddess Diana, and of the image which fell down from Jupiter?

Act 19:35

Seeing then that these things cannot be spoken against, ye ought to be quiet, and to do nothing rashly.

Act 19:36

For ye have brought hither these men, which are neither robbers of churches, nor yet blasphemers of your goddess.

Act 19:37

Wherefore if Demetrius, and the craftsmen which are with him, have a matter against any man, the law is open, and there are deputies: let them implead one another.

Act 19:38

But if ye enquire anything concerning other matters, it shall be determined in a lawful assembly.

Act 19:39

For we are in danger to be called in question for this day's uproar, there being no cause whereby we may give an account of this concourse.

Act 19:40

And when he had thus spoken, he dismissed the assembly.

Act 19:41

Christianity was beginning to take hold in Ephesus, and a certain man by the name of Demetrius began to cause confusion or uncertainty among the people; by the time Paul got there, he could not speak because of the confusion that was made. So, a man by the name of Alexander calmed the people down and dismissed them.

It just takes one person to cause confusion. Just recently, me and my wife were in church, and when you think you've seen it all, something new always happens.

Nevertheless, as we were listening to the Pastor preach the truth, he stated, “Try me, Lord, try me.” Little did the Pastor know that at the end of his sermon, a woman began to argue out loud and defend the sins she was committing.

Thus, she tried to cause confusion in the church and for the Pastor. The Pastor went through the quickest trial he asked for but he handled the situation very well. When we say try me, Lord, then get yourself ready for a trial. Paul tells us this in 1 Corinthians 14:33

For God is not the author of confusion, but of peace, as in all churches of the saints.

When people cause disorder in a church, it is not of God.

What causes disorder in the church among the people?

1 Corinthians 3: 1-4

And I, brethren, could not speak unto you as unto spiritual, but as unto carnal, even as unto babes in Christ.

1Co 3:1

I have fed you with milk, and not with meat: for hitherto ye were not able to bear it, neither yet now are ye able.

1Co 3:2

For ye are yet carnal: for whereas there is among you envying, and strife, and divisions, are ye not carnal, and walk as men?

1Co 3:3

For while one saith, I am of Paul; and another, I am of Apollos; are ye not carnal?

1Co 3:4

When people fall into the lust of the flesh, there will be envy, strife, and then division.

There is nothing that will make you any sicker than church trouble.

When pride, jealousy, and gossip begin in the church, then you can encounter confusion. This is what we call carnality. We will address this subject in a later chapter.

Just how do we attack confusion? Simple, keeping one gate closed and two gates open. What does it mean? You may ask me. Keep on reading; we will learn a lesson or two.

We have already talked about some of the gossip in an earlier chapter, but I like to go deeper into this subject. When a person learns to keep their mouth shut (the one gate closed) and their ears open, in this way you will learn something. Just one word can cause confusion and even could split a whole church. As Christians, let us learn what a bridle is on our tongue.

An older Sister in the church told me, "Brother Sam, if we disagree on a subject, let us put it on the shelf, for in the end, we will find out who is right, or we both could be wrong. So, let us learn to get along and not cause confusion.

Follow peace with all men, and holiness, without which no man shall see the Lord:

Heb 12:14

Chapter 8 Attack on Falsehood

In the first book I wrote, "The Shepherd and the Wolf," I spoke of false doctrine, false prophets, and hirelings. In this chapter, I like to discuss how to attack the falsehood of a wolf in sheep's clothing.

Did the church, in the beginning, have false men and women? Yes, the church did. Let us look at how these were taken care of then and what to do now.In

Matthew 24:23-26,

Then if any man shall say unto you, Lo, here is Christ, or there; believe it not.

Mat 24:23

For there shall arise false Christs and false prophets, and shall shew great signs and wonders; insomuch that, if it were possible, they shall deceive the very elect.

Mat 24:24

Behold, I have told you before.

Mat 24:25

Wherefore if they shall say unto you, Behold, he is in the desert; go not forth: behold, he is in the secret chambers; believe it not.

Mat 24:26

Jesus was warning his disciples to not follow after the false Christ and false prophets. The words of Jesus still hold true today.

Looking at verse 25, Jesus said he had told them before. Jesus was preparing his disciples.

Looking at verse 26, Jesus knew he would be raised from the grave of death.

So, Jesus said not to look for him in the desert or in secret chambers. Jesus knew that publicly, he would be raised from death. As Christians, we do not hide that we follow Jesus. There is no such thing as a secret in Christianity. You are saved, or you are not saved. Let us look at.

Matthew 10:32-33

Whosoever, therefore, shall confess me before men, him will I confess also before my Father which is in heaven.

Mat 10:32

But whosoever shall deny me before men, him will I also deny before my Father which is in heaven.

Mat 10:33

So, are you going to take a stand for Jesus? Or deny him? Are you going to be the winner? Or a loser?

How does God deal with falsehood? Let us look in

Leviticus 10:1-10,

And Nadab and Abihu, the sons of Aaron, took either of them his censer, and put fire therein, and put incense thereon, and offered strange fire before the LORD, which he commanded them not.

Lev 10:1

And there went out fire from the LORD, and devoured them, and they died before the LORD.

Lev 10:2

Then Moses said unto Aaron, This is it that the LORD spake, saying, I will be sanctified in them that come nigh me, and before all the people I will be glorified. And Aaron held his peace.

Lev 10:3

And Moses called Mishael and Elzaphan, the sons of Uzziel the uncle of Aaron, and said unto them, Come near, carry your brethren from before the sanctuary out of the camp.

Lev 10:4

So, they went near, and carried them in their coats out of the camp; as Moses had said.

Lev 10:5

And Moses said unto Aaron, and unto Eleazar and unto Ithamar, his sons, Uncover not your heads, neither rend your clothes; lest ye die, and lest wrath come upon all the people: but let your brethren, the whole house of Israel, bewail the burning which the LORD hath kindled.

Lev 10:6

And ye shall not go out from the door of the tabernacle of the congregation, lest ye die: for the anointing oil of the LORD is upon you. And they did according to the word of Moses.

Lev 10:7

And the LORD spake unto Aaron, saying,

Lev 10:8

Do not drink wine nor strong drink, thou, nor thy sons with thee, when ye go into the tabernacle of the congregation, lest ye die: it shall be a statute forever throughout your generations:

Lev 10:9

And that ye may put difference between holy and unholy, and between unclean and clean;

Lev 10:10

And that ye may teach the children of Israel all the statutes which the LORD hath spoken unto them by the hand of Moses.

Lev 10:11

Nadab and Abihu were chosen by God to do service unto the Lord. They did their jobs well until they disobeyed God and offered a strange fire unto the Lord. The true fire of God devoured them.

Today in many churches, there is strange fire (teachings). These teachings are leading men into hell by the numbers. Looking at

Jeremiah 5:11-14,

For the house of Israel and the house of Judah have dealt very

treacherously against me, saith the LORD.

Jer 5:11

They have belied the LORD and said, It is not he; neither shall evil come upon us; neither shall we see sword nor famine:

Jer 5:12

And the prophets shall become wind, and the word is not in them: thus shall it be done unto them.

Jer 5:13

Wherefore thus saith the LORD God of hosts, Because ye speak this word, behold, I will make my words in thy mouth fire, and this people wood, and it shall devour them.

Jer 5:14

The house of Israel and Judah walked away from the Lord; they went after other Gods. The prophets began to lie unto them, and their words became swift of air and became no use. God said that his words would become as of fire and the people as of wood, for they would be devoured. It takes the Spirit of God to deal with false teachings. When you hear a teaching that does not line up with the Word of God (KJV), then run from that teaching. That is why we must study the Word of God and pray that God will show us the meaning. If the pastor is a Man of God, he will correct the teaching of the false prophet and warn his flock.

One man alone stood the test of time when all the laws of the land changed. This man came through the greatest trial of his life. Let us look at

Daniel 6,

It pleased Darius to set over the kingdom a hundred and twenty princes, which should be over the whole kingdom;

Dan 6:1

And over these three presidents; of whom Daniel was first: that the princes might give accounts unto them, and the king should have no

damage.

Dan 6:2

Then this Daniel was preferred above the presidents and princes because an excellent spirit was in him; and the king thought to set him over the whole realm.

Dan 6:3

Then the presidents and princes sought to find occasion against Daniel concerning the kingdom, but they could find none occasion nor fault; forasmuch as he was faithful, neither was there any error or fault found in him.

Dan 6:4

Then said these men, We shall not find any occasion against this Daniel, except we find it against him concerning the law of his God.

Dan 6:5

Then these presidents and princes assembled together to the king, and said thus unto him, King Darius, live forever.

Dan 6:6

All the presidents of the kingdom, the governors, and the princes, the counsellors, and the captains have consulted together to establish a royal statute, and to make a firm decree, that whosoever shall ask a petition of any God or man for thirty days, save of thee, O king, he shall be cast into the den of lions.

Dan 6:7

Now, O king, establish the decree, and sign the writing, that it be not changed, according to the law of the Medes and Persians, which altereth not.

Dan 6:8

Wherefore King Darius signed the writing and the decree.

Dan 6:9

Now when Daniel knew that the writing was signed, he went into his house; and his windows being open in his chamber toward Jerusalem, he kneeled upon his knees three times a day and prayed, and gave thanks before his God, as he did aforetime.

Dan 6:10

Then these men assembled and found Daniel praying and making supplication before his God.

Dan 6:11

Then they came near, and spake before the king concerning the king's decree; Hast thou not signed a decree, that every man that shall ask a petition of any God or man within thirty days, save of thee, O king, shall be cast into the den of lions? The king answered and said, The thing is true, according to the law of the Medes and Persians, which altereth not.

Dan 6:12

Then answered they and said before the king, That Daniel, which is of the children of the captivity of Judah, regardeth not thee, O king, nor the decree that thou hast signed, but maketh his petition three times a day.

Dan 6:13

Then the king, when he heard these words, was sore displeased with himself, and set his heart on Daniel to deliver him: and he laboured till the going down of the sun to deliver him.

Dan 6:14

Then these men assembled unto the king, and said unto the king, Know, O king, that the law of the Medes and Persians is, That no decree nor statute which the king establisheth may be changed.

Dan 6:15

Then the king commanded, and they brought Daniel, and cast him into the den of lions. Now the king spake and said unto Daniel, Thy God whom thou servest continually, he will deliver thee.

Dan 6:16

And a stone was brought, and laid upon the mouth of the den, and the king sealed it with his own signet, and with the signet of his lords; that the purpose might not be changed concerning Daniel.

Dan 6:17

Then the king went to his palace, and passed the night fasting: neither were instruments of musick brought before him: and his sleep went from him.

Dan 6:18

Then the king arose very early in the morning and went in haste unto the den of lions.

Dan 6:19

And when he came to the den, he cried with a lamentable voice unto Daniel: and the king spake and said to Daniel, O Daniel, servant of the living God, is thy God, whom thou servest continually, able to deliver thee from the lions?

Dan 6:20

Then said Daniel unto the king, O king, live forever.

Dan 6:21

My God hath sent his angel, and hath shut the lions' mouths, that they have not hurt me: forasmuch as before him innocency was found in me; and also before thee, O king, have I done no hurt.

Dan 6:22

Then was the king exceeding glad for him, and commanded that they should take Daniel up out of the den. So, Daniel was taken up out of the den, and no manner of hurt was found upon him, because he believed in his God.

Dan 6:23

And the king commanded, and they brought those men which had accused Daniel, and they cast them into the den of lions, them, their children, and their wives; and the lions had the mastery of them, and brake all their bones in pieces or ever they came at the bottom of the den.

Dan 6:24

Then king Darius wrote unto all people, nations, and languages, that dwell in all the earth; Peace be multiplied unto you.

Dan 6:25

I make a decree, That in every dominion of my kingdom, men tremble and fear before the God of Daniel: for he is the living God, and stedfast forever, and his kingdom that which shall not be destroyed, and his dominion shall be even unto the end.

Dan 6:26

He delivereth and rescueth, and he worketh signs and wonders in heaven and in earth, who hath delivered Daniel from the power of the lions.

Dan 6:27

So, this Daniel prospered in the reign of Darius, and in the reign of Cyrus the Persian.

Dan 6:28

Daniel went through a test of times and the laws of the land had changed. The leaders tried to deceive Daniel into not praying three times a day, but Daniel, with all his faith in God, said, I will pray. I will keep my trust in God.

So as before, Daniel went out to pray. The wicked men caught him and accused him, and had him thrown into the den of lions. But wait, there was one man who knew that Daniel's God was real. This man, this worldly King Darius, begins to fast and pray.

When Daniel walked into the den of lions, the angel was already there and had the lion's mouth shut.

The king saw who was real and who was false. The men who caused havoc for Daniel and their whole families were cast in the den of lions.

To find the false and to attack the false takes time. As we pastored this one church, the deacon wanted to hold church in one hand and hold casinos in the other hand. Yes, casinos are a sin. So, I began to ask God how to expose this man for what he really was.

So, in time, with prayer and fasting, this man exposed himself as to who he really was. So, one night, The Holy Ghost came on the scene, and a message was brought forth to this man to choose whom he wanted to serve. Sad to say, this man went the way of the world. God gave him a chance to repent but he chose to follow the lust of his heart.

We, as Christians, must attack falsehood at its core before it begins. Proverbs 14:12 tells us this,

There is a way which seemeth right unto a man but the end thereof are the ways of death.

This Scripture is so important that it is found again in 16:25. So what is the right way? The way is Jesus Christ and the cross. Looking at Romans 6:20-21,

For when ye were the servants of sin, ye were free from righteousness.

Rom 6:20

What fruit had ye then in those things whereof ye are now ashamed? for the end of those things is death.

Rom 6:21

When we as sinners severed sin, but after Salvation, we serve Christ. We will not be ashamed of Jesus. Thus, we attack Falsehood.

Chapter 9 Attacking Hypocrisies

What is hypocrisy? A pretender. To be what, one is not. Peter brings out an interesting thought.

Wherefore laying aside all malice, and all guile, and hypocrisies, and envies, and all evil speakings,

1Pe 2:1

As newborn babes, desire the sincere milk of the word, that ye may grow thereby:

1Pe 2:2

If so be ye have tasted that the Lord is gracious.

1Pe 2:3

Here Peter brings out malice, guile, hypocrisy, envy and all the evil speaking.

Malice means to hurt others, Guile means to be deceitful and hypocrisy means being a pretender.

We, as Christians, must lay aside these sins. When a person goes into a church with the intent to cause trouble, confusion, and strife, then that person becomes a hypocrite.

Peter is warning us to stay away and be like a newborn baby and desire the sincere milk of the word. Sincere means to be clean, without deceit, and be genuine.

Once, I went to a furniture store to buy a leather couch. It looked like leather, felt like leather. So, I bought the couch by the word of the store seller that it was genuine leather. I got it home, and within six months, the couch began to crack and peel off. It was not real leather but a fake. I was not pleased. I learned to watch what I buy at that store. This is called hypocrisy, to say or pretend to be something that is not true. Hypocrites will deceive you for just a few dollars.

Where do you find hypocrisies? You can find it; on the job, in politics, and mostly in church. Hypocrites are very religious. What did Jesus say about hypocrites?

Take heed that ye do not your alms before men, to be seen of them: otherwise, ye have no reward of your Father which is in heaven.

Mat 6:1

Therefore when thou doest thine alms, do not sound a trumpet before thee, as the hypocrites do in the synagogues and in the streets, that they may have glory of men. Verily I say unto you, They have their reward.

Mat 6:2

But when thou doest alms, let not thy left hand know what thy right-hand doeth:

Mat 6:3

That thine alms may be in secret: and thy Father which seeth in secret himself shall reward thee openly.

Mat 6:4

And when thou prayest, thou shalt not be as the hypocrites are: for they love to pray standing in the synagogues and in the corners of the streets, that they may be seen of men. Verily I say unto you, They have their reward.

Mat 6:5

But thou, when thou prayest, enter into thy closet, and when thou hast shut thy door, pray to thy Father which is in secret; and thy Father which seeth in secret shall reward thee openly.

Mat 6:6

But when ye pray, use not vain repetitions, as the heathen do: for they think that they shall be heard for their much speaking.

Mat 6:7

Be not ye, therefore, like unto them: for your Father knoweth what things ye have need of before ye ask him.

Mat 6:8

A hypocrite likes to be seen and to be heard. They like to draw attention to themselves and not to Jesus.

Jesus pronounced eight woes unto the scribes, Pharisees, and hypocrites.

Then spake Jesus to the multitude, and to his disciples,

Mat 23:1

Saying, The scribes and the Pharisees sit in Moses' seat:

Mat 23:2

All therefore whatsoever they bid you observe, that observe and do; but do not ye after their works: for they say, and do not.

Mat 23:3

For they bind heavy burdens and grievous to be borne and lay them on men's shoulders; but they themselves will not move them with one of their fingers.

Mat 23:4

But all their works they do for to be seen of men: they make broad their phylacteries, and enlarge the borders of their garments,

Mat 23:5

And love the uppermost rooms at feasts and the chief seats in the synagogues,

Mat 23:6

And greetings in the markets, and to be called of men, Rabbi, Rabbi.

Mat 23:7

But be not ye called Rabbi: for one is your Master, even Christ; and all ye are brethren.

Mat 23:8

And call no man your father upon the earth: for one is your Father, which is in heaven.

Mat 23:9

Neither be ye called masters: for one is your Master, even Christ.

Mat 23:10

But he that is greatest among you shall be your servant.

Mat 23:11

And whosoever shall exalt himself shall be abased, and he that shall humble himself shall be exalted.

Mat 23:12

But woe unto you, scribes and Pharisees, hypocrites! for ye shut up the kingdom of heaven against men: for ye neither go in yourselves, neither suffer ye them that are entering to go in.

Mat 23:13

Woe unto you, scribes and Pharisees, hypocrites! for ye devour widows' houses, and for a pretence make long prayer: therefore ye shall receive the greater damnation.

Mat 23:14

Woe unto you, scribes and Pharisees, hypocrites! For ye compass sea and land to make one proselyte, and when he is made, ye make him twofold more the child of hell than yourselves.

Mat 23:15

Woe unto you, ye blind guides, which say, Whosoever, shall swear by the temple, it is nothing; but whosoever shall swear by the gold of the temple, he is a debtor!

Mat 23:16

Ye fools and blind: for whether is greater, the gold, or the temple that sanctifieth the gold?

Mat 23:17

And, Whosoever, shall swear by the altar, it is nothing; but whosoever sweareth by the gift that is upon it, he is guilty.

Mat 23:18

Ye fools and blind: for whether is greater, the gift, or the altar that sanctifieth the gift?

Mat 23:19

Whoso therefore, shall swear by the altar, sweareth by it, and by all things thereon.

Mat 23:20

And whoso shall swear by the temple, sweareth by it, and by him that dwelleth therein.

Mat 23:21

And he that shall swear by heaven, sweareth by the throne of God, and by him that sitteth thereon.

Mat 23:22

Woe unto you, scribes and Pharisees, hypocrites! for ye pay tithe of mint and anise and cummin, and have omitted the weightier matters of the law, judgment, mercy, and faith: these ought ye to have done, and not to leave the other undone.

Mat 23:23

Ye blind guides, which strain at a gnat, and swallow a camel.

Mat 23:24

Woe unto you, scribes and Pharisees, hypocrites! For ye make clean the outside of the cup and of the platter, but within they are full of extortion and excess.

Mat 23:25

Thou blind Pharisee, cleanse first that which is within the cup and platter, that the outside of them may be clean also.

Mat 23:26

Woe unto you, scribes and Pharisees, hypocrites! for ye are like unto whited sepulchres, which indeed appear beautiful outward, but are within full of dead men's bones, and of all uncleanness.

Mat 23:27

Even so, ye also outwardly appear righteous unto men, but within ye are full of hypocrisy and iniquity.

Mat 23:28

Woe unto you, scribes and Pharisees, hypocrites! because ye build the tombs of the prophets and garnish the sepulchres of the righteous,

Mat 23:29

And say, If we had been in the days of our fathers, we would not have been partakers with them in the blood of the prophets.

Mat 23:30

Wherefore ye be witnesses unto yourselves, that ye are the children of them which killed the prophets.

Mat 23:31

Fill ye up then the measure of your fathers.

Mat 23:32

Ye serpents, ye generation of vipers, how can ye escape the damnation of hell?

Mat 23:33

Wherefore, behold, I send unto you prophets and wise men, and scribes: and some of them ye shall kill and crucify; and some of them shall ye scourge in your synagogues, and persecute them from city to city:

Mat 23:34

That upon you may come all the righteous blood shed upon the earth, from the blood of righteous Abel unto the blood of Zacharias son of Barachias, whom ye slew between the temple and the altar.

Mat 23:35

Verily I say unto you, All these things shall come upon this generation.

Mat 23:36

I believe Jesus spoke this very plain and clear. Jesus also said this in

Luke 12:1-3

In the meantime, when there were gathered together an innumerable multitude of people, insomuch that they trode one upon another, he began to say unto his disciples first of all, Beware ye of the leaven of the Pharisees, which is hypocrisy.

Luk 12:1

For there is nothing covered, that shall not be revealed; neither hid, that shall not be known.

Luk 12:2

Therefore, whatsoever ye have spoken in darkness shall be heard in the light; and that which ye have spoken in the ear in closets shall be proclaimed upon the housetops.

Luk 12:3

A person who goes to church and proclaims one thing and lives another way out of the church, living like this will also make one a hypocrite. For example, a preacher preaches that it is a sin to own a TV, but he himself has one in his bedroom and hides it from people to see. This preacher just made himself a hypocrite. It is what is in the heart that can make one a hypocrite.

Judge not, that ye be not judged.

Mat 7:1

For with what judgment ye judge, ye shall be judged: and with what measure ye mete, it shall be measured to you again.

Mat 7:2

And why beholdest thou the mote that is in thy brother's eye, but considerest not the beam that is in thine own eye?

Mat 7:3

Or how wilt thou say to thy brother, Let me pull out the mote out of

thine eye; and, behold, a beam is in thine own eye?

Mat 7:4

Thou hypocrite, first cast out the beam out of thine own eye, and then shalt thou see clearly to cast out the mote out of thy brother's eye.

Mat 7:5

I like to ask you this "Where is your heart?" For what is in the heart will come out.

So how do we attack hypocrisies in the church and in our lives? With Just two words, "LIVE RIGHT". If this issue is not dealt with in our church, then our churches are in trouble. At the close of this, I want to say what Paul said in

Galatians 5:24-26.

And they that are Christ's have crucified the flesh with the affections and lusts.

Gal 5:24

If we live in the Spirit, let us also walk in the Spirit.

Gal 5:25

Let us not be desirous of vain glory, provoking one another, envying one another.

Gal 5:26

Chapter 10 Attack on Carnality

Carnal means the fleshly desires of the heart. 1 Corinthians 3:1-4 tells us this, And I, brethren, could not speak unto you as unto spiritual, but as unto carnal, even as unto babes in Christ.

1Co 3:1

I have fed you with milk, and not with meat: for hitherto ye were not able to bear it, neither yet now are ye able.

1Co 3:2

For ye are yet carnal: for whereas there is among you envying, and strife, and divisions, are ye not carnal, and walk as men?

1Co 3:3

For while one saith, I am of Paul; and another, I am of Apollos; are ye not carnal?

1Co 3:4

As a baby in Christ, we start on the milk, and as we grow, we get on the meat.

There are some Christians out there that have been in church for forty years and are still on the bottle drinking a watered-down gospel. They have envy, strife, and in some cases, divisions. St. Paul brings out how we become carnal when we follow man and not God.

Let us look at this from a pastor's point of view. Me and my wife was a Pastor of this one church. The church grew and doing well; in time to come, the Lord led us to resign. As I was packing my things out of my office, some of the people from church came to me and said, Bro. Sam, if you will find another building, we will start a church there. I stopped what I was doing; this was my reply, "Brother, I came here to see the church grow and build-up, and it has; I ask that you and the others stay here and follow Jesus and to build the church up. They stayed there, and the church grew.

When we as Christians begin to follow the preacher, then we go from spiritual to carnal. A Preacher, man or woman, will always fall and come short of the glory of God. When we follow Jesus, we will not fall. I like to bring out a point; people will get to that end in Church where they will have the attitude of "us four and no more". When we get to this end, we become carnal and not spiritual. When we cease to grow spiritually, then there is one other way to the carnal ways.

We must fight, war, and attack carnality every day. Yes, there are laws that are temporal, meaning just for a season. Then there are laws that are perpetual, meaning, set in stone. This part of carnal thoughts and deeds are done every day. Let us look at some of the laws that are set in stone.

And the LORD spake unto Moses, saying,

Lev 18:1

Speak unto the children of Israel, and say unto them, I am the LORD your God.

Lev 18:2

After the doings of the land of Egypt, wherein ye dwelt, shall ye not do: and after the doings of the land of Canaan, whither I bring you, shall ye not do: neither shall ye walk in their ordinances.

Lev 18:3

Ye shall do my judgments, and keep mine ordinances, to walk therein: I am the LORD your God.

Lev 18:4

Ye shall therefore keep my statutes and my judgments: which if a man do, he shall live in them: I am the LORD.

Lev 18:5

None of you shall approach to any that is near of kin to him, to uncover their nakedness: I am the LORD.

Lev 18:6

The nakedness of thy father, or the nakedness of thy mother, shalt thou not uncover: she is thy mother; thou shalt not uncover her nakedness.

Lev 18:7

The nakedness of thy father's wife shalt thou not uncover: it is thy father's nakedness.

Lev 18:8

The nakedness of thy sister, the daughter of thy father, or daughter of thy mother, whether she be born at home, or born abroad, even their nakedness thou shalt not uncover.

Lev 18:9

The nakedness of thy son's daughter, or of thy daughter's daughter, even their nakedness thou shalt not uncover: for theirs is thine own nakedness.

Lev 18:10

The nakedness of thy father's wife's daughter, begotten of thy father, she is thy sister, thou shalt not uncover her nakedness.

Lev 18:11

Thou shalt not uncover the nakedness of thy father's sister: she is thy father's near kinswoman.

Lev 18:12

Thou shalt not uncover the nakedness of thy mother's sister: for she is thy mother's near kinswoman.

Lev 18:13

Thou shalt not uncover the nakedness of thy father's brother, thou shalt not approach to his wife: she is thine aunt.

Lev 18:14

Thou shalt not uncover the nakedness of thy daughter-in-law: she is thy son's wife; thou shalt not uncover her nakedness.

Lev 18:15

Thou shalt not uncover the nakedness of thy brother's wife: it is thy brother's nakedness.

Lev 18:16

Thou shalt not uncover the nakedness of a woman and her daughter, neither shalt thou take her son's daughter, or her daughter's daughter, to uncover her nakedness; for they are her near kinswomen: it is wickedness.

Lev 18:17

Neither shalt thou take a wife to her sister, to vex her, to uncover her nakedness, beside the other in her lifetime.

Lev 18:18

Also, thou shalt not approach unto a woman to uncover her nakedness, as long as she is put apart for her uncleanness.

Lev 18:19

Moreover, thou shalt not lie carnally with thy neighbour's wife, to defile thyself with her.

Lev 18:20

And thou shalt not let any of thy seed pass through the fire to Molech, neither shalt thou profane the name of thy God: I am the LORD.

Lev 18:21

Thou shalt not lie with mankind, as with womankind: it is an abomination.

Lev 18:22

Neither shalt thou lie with any beast to defile thyself therewith: neither shall any woman stand before a beast to lie down thereto: it is confusion.

Lev 18:23

Defile not ye yourselves in any of these things: for in all these the nations are defiled which I cast out before you:

Lev 18:24

And the land is defiled: therefore, I do visit the iniquity thereof upon it, and the land itself vomiteth out her inhabitants.

Lev 18:25

Ye shall therefore keep my statutes and my judgments, and shall not commit any of these abominations; neither any of your own nation nor any stranger that sojourneth among you:

Lev 18:26

(For all these abominations have the men of the land done, which were before you, and the land is defiled;)

Lev 18:27

That the land spue not you out also, when ye defile it, as it spued out the nations that were before you.

Lev 18:28

For whosoever shall commit any of these abominations, even the souls that commit them shall be cut off from among their people.

Lev 18:29

Therefore, shall ye keep mine ordinance, that ye commit not any one of these abominable customs, which were committed before you, and that ye defile not yourselves therein: I am the LORD your God.

Lev 18:30

God begins to tell us what incest is and how sinful or carnal this sin is. Looking at verse 20, God says it is carnal or meaning the desire of the flesh. Then God goes on down in the scripture how homosexuality, bestiality, is a SIN. Church, any nation that allows this to be gone, then on Judgment Day they will stand before God.

How is a Christian to attack carnality? To attack, let us use the word of God.

Therefore, brethren, we are debtors, not to the flesh, to live after the flesh.

Rom 8:12

For if ye live after the flesh, ye shall die: but if ye through the Spirit do mortify the deeds of the body, ye shall live.

Rom 8:13

For though I be absent in the flesh, yet am I with you in the spirit, joying and beholding your order, and the stedfastness of your faith in Christ.

Col 2:5

As ye have therefore received Christ Jesus the Lord, so walk ye in him:

Col 2:6

Rooted and built up in him, and stablished in the faith, as ye have been taught, abounding therein with thanksgiving.

Col 2:7

Beware lest any man spoil you through philosophy and vain deceit, after the tradition of men, after the rudiments of the world, and not after Christ.

Col 2:8

For in him dwelleth all the fulness of the Godhead bodily.

Col 2:9

Mortify, what does mortify mean? To put to death,

2 Corinthians 5:17

Therefore, if any man be in Christ, he is a new creature: old things are passed away; behold, all things are become new.

When we come to Jesus Christ, old things will die out. We must repent, meaning to turn away from sin. So, to mortify the flesh and to kill the flesh, our soul, our spiritual being, comes alive in Jesus. Looking at

Col 3:10-7,

And have put on the new man, which is renewed in knowledge after the image of him that created him:

Col 3:10

Where there is neither Greek nor Jew, circumcision nor uncircumcision, Barbarian, Scythian, bond nor free: but Christ is all, and in all.

Col 3:11

Put on, therefore, as the elect of God, holy and beloved, bowels of mercies, kindness, humbleness of mind, meekness, longsuffering;

Col 3:12

Forbearing one another, and forgiving one another, if any man have a quarrel against any: even as Christ forgave you, so also do ye.

Col 3:13

And above all these things put on charity, which is the bond of perfectness.

Col 3:14

And let the peace of God rule in your hearts, to the which also ye are called in one body; and be ye thankful.

Col 3:15

Let the word of Christ dwell in you richly in all wisdom; teaching and admonishing one another in psalms and hymns and spiritual songs, singing with grace in your hearts to the Lord.

Col 3:16

And whatsoever ye do in word or deed, do all in the name of the Lord Jesus, giving thanks to God and the Father by him.

Col 3:17

We are to come alive in Christ Jesus. Looking Father in the scripture

Gal 5:13-26,

For, brethren, ye have been called unto liberty; only use not liberty for an occasion to the flesh, but by love serve one another.

Gal 5:13

For all the law is fulfilled in one word, even in this; Thou shalt love thy neighbour as thyself.

Gal 5:14

But if ye bite and devour one another, take heed that ye be not consumed one of another.

Gal 5:15

This I say then, Walk in the Spirit, and ye shall not fulfil the lust of the flesh.

Gal 5:16

For the flesh lusteth against the Spirit, and the Spirit against the flesh: and these are contrary the one to the other: so that ye cannot do the things that ye would.

Gal 5:17

But if ye be led of the Spirit, ye are not under the law.

Gal 5:18

Now the works of the flesh are manifest, which are these; Adultery, fornication, uncleanness, lasciviousness,

Gal 5:19

Idolatry, witchcraft, hatred, variance, emulations, wrath, strife, seditions, heresies,

Gal 5:20

Envyings, murders, drunkenness, revellings, and such like: of the which I tell you before, as I have also told you in time past, that they which do such things shall not inherit the kingdom of God.

Gal 5:21

But the fruit of the Spirit is love, joy, peace, longsuffering, gentleness, goodness, faith,

Gal 5:22

Meekness, temperance: against such there is no law.

Gal 5:23

And they that are Christ's have crucified the flesh with the affections and lusts.

Gal 5:24

If we live in the Spirit, let us also walk in the Spirit.

Gal 5:25

Let us not be desirous of vain glory, provoking one another, envying one another.

Gal 5:26

WOW! By walking in the Spirit of Jesus and by the love of God, we can mortify or attack carnality.

When we have the fruit of the Spirit, we become spiritually alive.

The word is not given to a non-believer but to a believer.

There will always be a war between the carnal and the Spiritual man.

The only way to Attack is to pray, study, and fast.

Chapter 11 Attacking Sin

We have covered just a few bases of sin, and we have learned to attack these sins, but they all are sins, and sin is a sin in God's eyes.

Just like a lie, a lie starts out with a seed, then it grows into something big, and eventually, the truth will come out. The truth will always set you free.

At the age of sixteen, I got my driving license. I wanted to go to church, and Mom wanted to go see her mother, so Dad said Sam take your mother to your grandmother's; then go to church and on your way back pick her up. As a teenager, that was like, WOW!

Anyhow, I got mom to grandma's, and I went on my way. I got into the city, and I made a red light turning left. Did not do it on purpose; it was an accident. I hit a truck with a cab full of people. I remember the first thing I did. I took my seat belt off and hit the pavement, and thank God no one was hurt. When the officer got there, I told him it was my fault and told him what had happened. I did not receive a ticket. Mom asked the officer why I did not get a ticket. He said That Sam told the truth. I found out then that telling the truth will always set you free.

What qualifies us to attack sin in the heat of the battle? We must have the whole Armour of God on

Ephesians 6:10-20,

Finally, my brethren, be strong in the Lord, and in the power of his might.

Eph 6:10

Put on the whole armour of God, that ye may be able to stand against the wiles of the devil.

Eph 6:11

For we wrestle not against flesh and blood, but against principalities, against powers, against the rulers of the darkness of this world, against spiritual wickedness in high places.

Eph 6:12

Wherefore take unto you the whole armour of God, that ye may be able to withstand in the evil day, and having done all, to stand.

Eph 6:13

Stand, therefore, having your loins girt about with truth, and having on the breastplate of righteousness;

Eph 6:14

And your feet shod with the preparation of the gospel of peace;

Eph 6:15

Above all, taking the shield of faith, wherewith ye shall be able to quench all the fiery darts of the wicked.

Eph 6:16

And take the helmet of salvation, and the sword of the Spirit, which is the word of God:

Eph 6:17

Praying always with all prayer and supplication in the Spirit, and watching thereunto with all perseverance and supplication for all saints;

Eph 6:18

And for me, that utterance may be given unto me, that I may open my mouth boldly, to make known the mystery of the gospel,

Eph 6:19

For which I am an ambassador in bonds: that therein I may speak boldly, as I ought to speak.

Eph 6:20

Paul tells us Finally, I have told you, listen, we must be strong in the Lord and in the power of His Might.

What is the power of His Might? Jesus told his disciples this,

And, being assembled together with them, commanded them that they

should not depart from Jerusalem, but wait for the promise of the Father, which, saith he, ye have heard of me.

Act 1:4

For John truly baptized with water; but ye shall be baptized with the Holy Ghost not many days henceforth

Act 1:5

When they therefore were come together, they asked of him, saying, Lord, wilt thou at this time restore again the kingdom to Israel?

Act 1:6

And he said unto them, It is not for you to know the times or the seasons, which the Father hath put in his own power.

Act 1:7

But ye shall receive power, after that the Holy Ghost is come upon you: and ye shall be witnesses unto me both in Jerusalem, and in all Judaea, and in Samaria, and unto the uttermost part of the earth.

Act 1:8

Look at what Jesus said, ye shall receive power, after that the Holy Ghost is come upon you. Jesus was not speaking to just twelve men, there were one hundred and twenty people there.

Acts 1:12-15,

Then returned they unto Jerusalem from the mount called Olivet, which is from Jerusalem a sabbath day's journey.

Act 1:12

And when they were come in, they went up into an upper room, where abode both Peter, and James, and John, and Andrew, Philip, and Thomas, Bartholomew, and Matthew, James the son of Alphaeus, and Simon Zelotes, and Judas the brother of James.

Act 1:13

These all continued with one accord in prayer and supplication, with the women, and Mary the mother of Jesus, and with his brethren.

Act 1:14

And in those days Peter stood up in the midst of the disciples, and said, (the number of names together were about a hundred and twenty,)

Act 1:15

With a hundred and twenty gathered in the upper room, they were waiting for the power from on high.

Acts 2:1-8,

And when the day of Pentecost was fully come, they were all with one accord in one place.

Act 2:1

And suddenly there came a sound from heaven as of a rushing mighty wind, and it filled all the house where they were sitting.

Act 2:2

And there appeared unto them cloven tongues like as of fire, and it sat upon each of them.

Act 2:3

And they were all filled with the Holy Ghost, and began to speak with other tongues, as the Spirit gave them utterance.

Act 2:4

And there were dwelling at Jerusalem Jews, devout men, out of every nation under heaven.

Act 2:5

Now when this was noised abroad, the multitude came together and were confounded, because that every man heard them speak in his own language.

Act 2:6

And they were all amazed and marvelled, saying one to another, Behold, are not all these which speak Galilaeans?

Act 2:7

And how hear we every man in our own tongue, wherein we were born?

Act 2:8

WOW! Did you get where the power was? The Holy Ghost came and settled into them, and they began to speak in other tongues. The Apostle Peter, now filled with the Holy Ghost, began to speak to them.

Look at verse 6, "NOW WHEN THIS WAS NOSIED ABROAD." There was no quietness as we see it in today's churches, but there was power; there was shouting, preaching, and speaking in other tongues. This is baptismal of the Holy Ghost, the comforter that Jesus spoke about in

John 16:5-16,

But now I go my way to him that sent me; and none of you asketh me, Whither goest thou?

John 16:5

But because I have said these things unto you, sorrow hath filled your heart.

John 16:6

Nevertheless, I tell you the truth; It is expedient for you that I go away: for if I go not away, the Comforter will not come unto you; but if I depart, I will send him unto you.

John 16:7

And when he is come, he will reprove the world of sin, and of righteousness, and of judgment: Of sin, because they believe not on me;

Joh 16:9

Of righteousness, because I go to my Father, and ye see me no more;

Joh 16:10

Of judgment, because the prince of this world is judged.

Joh 16:11

I have yet many things to say unto you, but ye cannot bear them now.

Joh 16:12

Howbeit when he, the Spirit of truth, is come, he will guide you into all truth: for he shall not speak of himself; but whatsoever he shall hear, that shall he speak: and he will shew you things to come.

Joh 16:13

He shall glorify me: for he shall receive of mine and shall shew it unto you.

Joh 16:14

All things that the Father hath are mine: therefore, said I, that he shall take of mine, and shall shew it unto you.

John 16:15

A little while, and ye shall not see me: and again, a little while, and ye shall see me, because I go to the Father.

John 16:16

So, the power is in the Holy Ghost. But wait, there is more; we also have the full Armour of God. Let us look more into this Armour. As Christians, we are in a Spiritual conflict called warfare of faith. Satan seeks out new ways to fight the church but the same sin. The sins of the old times are the same sins as today. Satan just uses the modern way to attack the church. It can be through phones, radios, TV, the internet; the list goes on and on. You see, these things are not sins. It is the way you use these things that can become a sin to you.

Let me give you some examples;

Gossip can be done on the phone, SIN. Radio can be listening to ungodly music, SIN. The TV, you can see anything off that thing; remember, your eyes are the window of your soul. Internet, once again, it is how you use it that it becomes a sin.

For some of the old timers out there, look at it this way. A haystack. Is the haystack sin? No, it is not. It is what goes on behind the haystack that becomes a sin. Hay is for the livestock to eat, but people have made it into another thing that pertains to sin.

Just like a wagon or car, they are not sinful unless you go to do sinful things.

A book is another form that can be used for sin; you can read in a book that has lust, greed, envy, strife, jealousy, murders, and hatred, and then all this comes even into view on TV. Should a Christian be reading these things or watching them on TV or the Internet? NO, all it does is plant a seed in someone's heart and allow it to grow.

It does not matter if you have been saved ten years or fifty years; each Christian will come up against sin in one form or another; rather, it is an old way or a new way; sin is sin.

To attack sin, we must be filled with the Holy Ghost and put on the whole Armour of God.

The Old Testament will always foreshadow the New Testament. Having said this, let us look at Isaiah concerning the Armour of God. Isaiah chapter 59 verses 16 through 21 tell us this,

And he saw that there was no man, and wondered that there was no intercessor: therefore, his arm brought salvation unto him; and his righteousness, it sustained him.

Isa 59:16

For he put on righteousness as a breastplate, and a helmet of salvation upon his head; and he put on the garments of vengeance for clothing, and was clad with zeal as a cloke.

Isa 59:17

According to their deeds, accordingly, he will repay, fury to his adversaries, recompence to his enemies; to the islands he will repay recompence.

Isa 59:18

So, shall they fear the name of the LORD from the west, and his glory from the rising of the sun. When the enemy shall come in like a flood, the Spirit of the LORD shall lift up a standard against him.

Isa 59:19

And the Redeemer shall come to Zion, and unto them that turn from transgression in Jacob, saith the LORD.

Isa 59:20

As for me, this is my covenant with them, saith the LORD; My spirit that is upon thee, and my words which I have put in thy mouth, shall not depart out of thy mouth, nor out of the mouth of thy seed, nor out of the mouth of thy seed's seed, saith the LORD, from henceforth and forever.

Isa 59:21

When looking at these verses, Paul is rehearsing what Isaiah said.

Paul expounds deeper into what the Armour of God is. In Eph 6:14-17, Paul is saying this; we need our lions to girt about with truth having on the breastplate of righteousness, our feet shod with the gospel of peace. We need Our shield of faith in the Lord Jesus Christ to quench the fiery darts of the wicked. We must be born again. There must be a change in our minds. Romans 12:1-2 says,

I beseech you therefore, brethren, by the mercies of God, that ye present your bodies a living sacrifice, holy, acceptable unto God, which is your reasonable service.

Rom 12:1

And be not conformed to this world: but be ye transformed by the renewing of your mind, that ye may prove what is that good, and acceptable, and perfect, will of God.

Rom 12:2

Then we need to know the word of God

For the word of God is quick, and powerful, and sharper than any two-edged sword, piercing even to the dividing asunder of soul and spirit, and of the joints and marrow, and is a discerner of the thoughts and intents of the heart.

Hebrews 4:12

The Bible is sharper than any two-edged sword. When the truth is being preached, it will cut going in and coming out. Every time you pick up the Word of God, he is speaking right to you.

All scripture is given by inspiration of God, and is profitable for doctrine, for reproof, for correction, for instruction in righteousness:

2 Timothy 3:16-17,

That the man of God may be perfect, thoroughly furnished unto all good works.

2Ti 3:17

We have the King James Version; the King James is the closest you can get to a translation of the Hebrew and Greek Scriptures. We have the scriptures; let us use them the way God wants them to be used for. There are so many versions out there, and if you follow the roots, it will lead you back to King James. Why? The King James is accreted of the scriptures.

Let us always Attack sin with the cross, the Armour, and with the love of God.

Chapter 12 There Is Hope

Hope is faith, faith is hope.

Now faith is the substance of things hoped for, the evidence of things not seen.

Hebrews 11:1

At the start of this book, I brought out the football game. When the team players come together they have hope in one another that they will win the game.

They practice the game day in and day out. They eat right, exercise right, study right. Even out of season, they are to practice.

At the beginning of the season, they have games to play and a bracket to follow. By winning each game they ascend on the bracket to the goal of winning. So, it is a must to have hope in one another to win the game and attain the trophy.

There is an incident that happened in the book of Acts 27:6-44 let us read into this incident.

And there the centurion found a ship of Alexandria sailing into Italy, and he put us therein.

Act 27:6

And when we had sailed slowly many days, and scarce were come over against Cnidus, the wind not suffering us, we sailed under Crete, over against Salmone;

Act 27:7

And, hardly passing it, came unto a place which is called The fair havens; nigh whereunto was the city of Lasea.

Act 27:8

Now when much time was spent, and when sailing was now dangerous, because the fast was now already past, Paul admonished them,

Act 27:9

And said unto them, Sirs, I perceive that this voyage will be with hurt and much damage, not only of the lading and ship but also of our lives.

Act 27:10

Nevertheless, the centurion believed the master and the owner of the ship, more than those things which were spoken by Paul.

Act 27:11

And because the haven was not commodious to winter in, the more part advised to depart thence also, if by any means they might attain to Phenice, and there to winter; which is a haven of Crete, and lieth toward the southwest and north-west.

Act 27:12

And when the south wind blew softly, supposing that they had obtained their purpose, loosing thence, they sailed close by Crete.

Act 27:13

But not long after there arose against it a tempestuous wind, called Euroclydon.

Act 27:14

And when the ship was caught, and could not bear up into the wind, we let her drive.

Act 27:15

And running under a certain island which is called Clauda, we had much work to come by the boat:

Act 27:16

When they had taken up, they used helps, undergirding the ship; and, fearing lest they should fall into the quicksands, strake sail, and so were driven.

Act 27:17

And we being exceedingly tossed with a tempest, the next day they lightened the ship;

Act 27:18

And the third day we cast out with our own hands the tackling of the ship.

Act 27:19

And when neither sun nor stars in many days appeared, and no small tempest lay on us, all hope that we should be saved was then taken away.

Act 27:20

But after long abstinence Paul stood forth in the midst of them, and said, Sirs, ye should have hearkened unto me, and not have loosed from Crete, and to have gained this harm and loss.

Act 27:21

And now I exhort you to be of good cheer: for there shall be no loss of any man's life among you, but of the ship.

Act 27:22

For there stood by me this night the angel of God, whose I am, and whom I serve,

Act 27:23

Saying, Fear not, Paul; thou must be brought before Caesar: and, lo, God hath given thee all them that sail with thee.

Act 27:24

Wherefore, sirs, be of good cheer: for I believe God, that it shall be even as it was told me.

Act 27:25

Howbeit we must be cast upon a certain island.

Act 27:26

But when the fourteenth night was come, as we were driven up and down in Adria, about midnight the shipmen deemed that they drew near to some country;

Act 27:27

And sounded, and found it twenty fathoms: and when they had gone a little further, they sounded again, and found it fifteen fathoms.

Act 27:28

Then fearing lest we should have fallen upon rocks, they cast four anchors out of the stern and wished for the day.

Act 27:29

And as the shipmen were about to flee out of the ship, when they had let down the boat into the sea, under colour as though they would have cast anchors out of the foreship,

Act 27:30

Paul said to the centurion and to the soldiers, Except these abide in the ship, ye cannot be saved.

Act 27:31

Then the soldiers cut off the ropes of the boat, and let her fall off.

Act 27:32

And while the day was coming on, Paul besought them all to take meat, saying, this day is the fourteenth day that ye have tarried and continued fasting, having taken nothing.

Act 27:33

Wherefore I pray you to take some meat: for this is for your health: for there shall not a hair fall from the head of any of you.

Act 27:34

And when he had thus spoken, he took bread, and gave thanks to God in presence of them all: and when he had broken it, he began to eat.

Act 27:35

Then were they all in good cheer, and they also took some meat.

Act 27:36

And we were in all in the ship two hundred threescore and sixteen souls.

Act 27:37

And when they had eaten enough, they lightened the ship and cast out the wheat into the sea.

Act 27:38

And when it was day, they knew not the land: but they discovered a certain creek with a shore, into which they were minded, if it were possible, to thrust in the ship.

Act 27:39

And when they had taken up the anchors, they committed themselves unto the sea and loosed the rudder bands, and hoised up the mainsail to the wind, and made toward shore.

Act 27:40

And falling into a place where two seas met, they ran the ship aground, and the forepart stuck fast, and remained unmoveable, but the hinder part was broken with the violence of the waves.

Act 27:41

And the soldiers' counsel was to kill the prisoners, lest any of them should swim out, and escape.

Act 27:42

But the centurion, willing to save Paul, kept them from their purpose; and commanded that they which could swim should cast themselves first into the sea, and get to land:

Act 27:43

And the rest, some on boards, and some on broken pieces of the ship. And so, it came to pass, that they escaped all safe to land.

Act 27:44

A lot of reading I know it is but, I want to bring out a point. They all pulled together and they all had hope and not a soul was lost.

The Church by having hope in one another can attack the enemy at full force and win. In whom do we put our hope in?

Romans 5:1-5,

Therefore, being justified by faith, we have peace with God through our Lord Jesus Christ:

Rom 5:1

By whom also we have access by faith into this grace wherein we stand, and rejoice in hope of the glory of God.

Rom 5:2

And not only so, but we glory in tribulations also: knowing that tribulation worketh patience;

Rom 5:3

And patience, experience; and experience, hope:

Rom 5:4

And hope maketh not ashamed; because the love of God is shed abroad in our hearts by the Holy Ghost which is given unto us.

Rom 5:5

Hope is in Jesus Christ. In tribulations, we can have our hope in Christ.

Hebrews 4:14-16 says this,

For we have not a high priest which cannot be touched with the feeling of our infirmities; but was in all points tempted like as we are, yet without sin.

Heb 4:15

Let us therefore come boldly unto the throne of grace, that we may obtain mercy, and find grace to help in time of need.

Heb 4:16

Jesus the Son of God, was tempted in all points but yet without sin. It is in Jesus Christ that we have this hope to come boldly unto the throne of grace and obtain mercy and help in times of trouble. King David said **Psa 71:1**

this best in the book of Psalms 71: 1-12

In thee, O LORD, do I put my trust: let me never be put to confusion.

Deliver me in thy righteousness, and cause me to escape: incline thine ear unto me, and save me.

Psa 71:2

Be thou my strong habitation, whereunto I may continually resort: thou hast given commandment to save me; for thou art my rock and my fortress.

Psa 71:3

Deliver me, O my God, out of the hand of the wicked, out of the hand of the unrighteous and cruel man.

Psa 71:4

For thou art my hope, O Lord GOD: thou art my trust from my youth.

Psa 71:5

By thee have I been holden up from the womb: thou art he that took me out of my mother's bowels: my praise shall be continually of thee.

Psa 71:6

am as a wonder unto many; but thou art my strong refuge.

Psa 71:7 I

Let my mouth be filled with thy praise and with thy honour all the day.

Psa 71:8

Cast me not off in the time of old age; forsake me not when my strength faileth.

Psa 71:9

For mine enemies speak against me, and they that lay wait for my soul take counsel together,

Psa 71:10

Saying, God hath forsaken him: persecute and take him; for there is none to deliver him.

Psa 71:11

O God, be not far from me: O my God, make haste for my help.

Psa 71:12

King David said, his hope is in the Lord. David goes on and tells us that happy is a man when he places his hope in the Lord. Psalms 146,

Praise ye the LORD. Praise the LORD, O my soul.

Psa 146:1

While I live will I praise the LORD: I will sing praises unto my God while I have any being.

Psa 146:2

Put not your trust in princes, nor in the son of man, in whom there is no help.

Psa 146:3

His breath goeth forth, he returneth to his earth; in that very day his thoughts perish.

Psa 146:4

Happy is he that hath the God of Jacob for his help, whose hope is in the LORD his God:

Psa 146:5

Which made heaven, and earth, the sea, and all that therein is: which keepeth truth forever:

Psa 146:6

Which executeth judgment for the oppressed: which giveth food to the hungry. The LORD looseth the prisoners:

Psa 146:7

The LORD openeth the eyes of the blind: the LORD raiseth them that are bowed down: the LORD loveth the righteous:

Psa 146:8

The LORD preserveth the strangers; he relieveth the fatherless and widow: but the way of the wicked he turneth upside down.

Psa 146:9

The LORD shall reign forever, even thy God, O Zion, unto all generations. Praise ye the LORD.

Psa 146:10

Notice, David said not to put your hope in man but in God.

Yes, we can attack with hope. Hope in the Father, hope in the Son and hope in the Holy Ghost. There is hope. Hope is faith, faith is in hope.

Chapter 13 There is no Turning Back

2 Timothy 4:6-8,

For I am now ready to be offered, and the time of my departure is at hand.

2Ti 4:6

I have fought a good fight, I have finished my course; I have kept the faith:

2Ti 4:7

Henceforth there is laid up for me a crown of righteousness, which the Lord, the righteous judge, shall give me at that day: and not to me only, but unto all them also that love his appearing.

2Ti 4:8

Apostle Paul was ready to go. There was no turning back. Paul knew that there was a heavenly peace waiting for him and for those who loved the appearance of the Lord Jesus Christ.

Paul also admonished Timothy to keep on fighting the good fight of faith.

Fight the good fight of faith, lay hold on eternal life, whereunto thou art also called, and hast professed a good profession before many witnesses.

1Ti 6:12

In this chapter, I would like to encourage Pastors, Teachers, Evangelists, and Singers not to give up.

I like to tell a trick that Satan tried on a Pastor to destroy his ministry and his work. The pastor had been holding revival meetings and Pastoring his Church. A woman in the church did not like what was going on, so she came up with a plan to frame this Man of God and ruin his ministry.

The Pastor and his wife came home really late to the meeting, and they received a phone call that one sister so and so was very badly sick and had requested the pastor to come and pray for her. It was very late; the Pastor was fixing to walk out the door, and the Holy Ghost said to take his wife. The Pastor said he argued with the Lord, but nevertheless, he turned around and asked his wife to join, and the Lord had to ask her to go. She went with her husband. As they went in, the woman was in bed, and she asked him to come into her bedroom, so he and his wife went into the room to pray for the sister. As they began to pray, the Holy Ghost fell on the pastor's wife, and she moved herself to the closet curtain, she opened the curtain, and behind the curtain was a man with a camera recording all that went on. They were going to frame this man, but God had other plans.

You see, when we obey God, then things will always work out for our good.

And we know that all things work together for good to them that love God, to them who are the called according to his purpose.

Romans 8:28

Once we get saved, Satan will do everything in his power to get us to turn back. In the church, there is no turning back. Now is the time to fight with all that you have. We have already spoken of the Armour of God. I say unto my Brother, I say unto my Sister, suit up; it's time for war.

The church is no recreation room, but it is the place to be ready to fight the world of sin. The church is no playhouse. Church is a place to prepare for the battle. You see, our service is not in the church, but service starts when you step outside the doors of the church. No! It is not a time to turn back; it is time to go forward with the prize before us. There is no turning back.

In today's society, Satan has attacked with all he has. Why? He knows he has just a short time. I want to look at a man that had No determination to turn back. His name is Job.

There was a man in the land of Uz, whose name was Job; and that man was perfect and upright, and one that feared God, and eschewed evil.

Job 1:1

And there were born unto him seven sons and three daughters.

Job 1:2

His substance also was seven thousand sheep, and three thousand camels, and five hundred yoke of oxen, and five hundred she asses, and a very great household; so that this man was the greatest of all the men of the East.

Job 1:3

And his sons went and feasted in their houses, everyone his day; and sent and called for their three sisters to eat and to drink with them.

Job 1:4

And it was so when the days of their feasting were gone about, that Job sent and sanctified them, and rose up early in the morning, and offered burnt offerings according to the number of them all: for Job said, It may be that my sons have sinned, and cursed God in their hearts. Thus, did Job continually.

Job 1:5

Now there was a day when the sons of God came to present themselves before the LORD, and Satan came also among them.

Job 1:6

And the LORD said unto Satan, Whence comest thou? Then Satan answered the LORD, and said, From going to and fro in the earth, and from walking up and down in it.

Job 1:7

And the LORD said unto Satan, Hast thou considered my servant Job, that there is none like him in the earth, a perfect and an upright man, one that feareth God, and escheweth evil?

Job 1:8

Then Satan answered the LORD, and said, Doth Job fear God for nought?

Job 1:9

Hast, not thou made a hedge about him, and about his house, and about all that he hath on every side? thou hast blessed the work of his hands, and his substance is increased in the land.

Job 1:10

But put forth thine hand now, and touch all that he hath, and he will curse thee to thy face.

Job 1:11

And the LORD said unto Satan, Behold, all that he hath is in thy power; only upon himself put not forth thine hand. So Satan went forth from the presence of the LORD.

Job 1:12

The Job ended up losing all he had. His kids, his wife, and his friends, who were not actually his true friends. Job never turned his back on God; he kept on living for the Lord. But in the end, God blessed him more than he ever had. Let us look at what God did.

Then Job answered the LORD, and said,

Job 42:1

I know that thou canst do everything and that no thought can be withholden from thee.

Job 42:2

Who is he that hideth counsel without knowledge? therefore have I uttered that I understood not; things too wonderful for me, which I knew not.

Job 42:3

Hear, I beseech thee, and I will speak: I will demand of thee, and declare thou unto me.

Job 42:4

I have heard of thee by the hearing of the ear: but now mine eye seeth thee.

Job 42:5

Wherefore I abhor myself, and repent in dust and ashes.

Job 42:6

And it was so, that after the LORD had spoken these words unto Job, the LORD said to Eliphaz the Temanite, My wrath is kindled against thee, and against thy two friends: for ye have not spoken of me the thing that is right, as my servant Job hath.

Job 42:7

Therefore, take unto you now seven bullocks and seven rams, and go to my servant Job, and offer up for yourselves a burnt offering; and my servant Job shall pray for you: for him will I accept: lest I deal with you after your folly, in that ye have not spoken of me the thing which is right, like my servant Job.

Job 42:8

So Eliphaz the Temanite and Bildad the Shuhite and Zophar the Naamathite went, and did according as the LORD commanded them: the LORD also accepted Job.

Job 42:9

And the LORD turned the captivity of Job when he prayed for his friends: also the LORD gave Job twice as much as he had before.

Job 42:10

Then came there unto him all his brethren, and all his sisters, and all they that had been of his acquaintance before, and did eat bread with him in his house: and they bemoaned him, and comforted him over all the evil that the LORD had brought upon him: every man also gave him a piece of money, and every one an earring of gold.

Job 42:11

So, the LORD blessed the latter end of Job more than his beginning: for he had fourteen thousand sheep, and six thousand camels, and a thousand yoke of oxen, and a thousand she asses.

Job 42:12

He had also seven sons and three daughters.

Job 42:13

And he called the name of the first, Jemima; and the name of the second, Kezia; and the name of the third, Kerenhappuch.

Job 42:14

And in all the land were no women found so fair as the daughters of Job: and their father gave them inheritance among their brethren.

Job 42:15

After this lived Job an hundred and forty years, and saw his sons, and his soans' sons, even four generations.

Job 42:16

So, Job died, being old and full of days.

Job 42:17

God blessed Job because he did not turn his back on God. But there was one man who did for thirty pieces of silver. His name is Judas Iscariot. What did he do?

Then Judas, which had betrayed him, when he saw that he was condemned, repented himself, and brought again the thirty pieces of silver to the chief priests and elders,

Mat 27:3

Saying, I have sinned in that I have betrayed the innocent blood. And they said, What is that to us? see thou to that.

Mat 27:4

And he cast down the pieces of silver in the temple and departed, and went and hanged himself.

Mat 27:5

And the chief priests took the silver pieces, and said, It is not lawful for to put them into the treasury, because it is the price of blood.

Mat 27:6

And they took counsel, and bought with them the potter's field, to bury strangers in.

Mat 27:7

Wherefore that field was called, The field of blood, unto this day.

Mat 27:8

Can a person backslide and go to hell? Yes, a person can. Can a Person come back to God? Yes, sure, look at Revelation with me.

Remember therefore from whence thou art fallen, and repent, and do the first works; or else I will come unto thee quickly, and will remove thy candlestick out of his place, except thou repent.

Rev 2:5

There is forgiveness; backsliders turn back to God and never look back again.

In the book of Revelation, the scriptures are telling us to be overcomers of sin. We are made more than conquerors.

Nay, in all these things we are more than conquerors through him that loved us.

Romans 8:37

We can win!! There is no time to turn back; let us go forward with victory.

Chapter 14 Attack with Commitment

These be the names of the mighty men whom David had: The Tachmonite that sat in the seat, chief among the captains; the same was Adino the Eznite: he lift up his spear against eight hundred, whom he slew at one time.

2Sam 23:8

And after him was Eleazar the son of Dodo the Ahohite, one of the three mighty men with David, when they defied the Philistines that were there gathered together to battle and the men of Israel were gone away:

2Sam 23:9

He arose and smote the Philistines until his hand was weary, and his hand clave unto the sword: and the LORD wrought a great victory that day, and the people returned after him only to spoil.

2Sam 23:10

And after him was Shammah the son of Agee the Hararite. And the Philistines were gathered together into a troop, where was a piece of ground full of lentiles: and the people fled from the Philistines.

2Sam 23:11

But he stood in the midst of the ground, and defended it, and slew the Philistines: and the LORD wrought a great victory.

2Sam 23:12

And three of the thirty chiefs went down, and came to David in the harvest time unto the cave of Adullam: and the troop of the Philistines pitched in the valley of Rephaim.

2Sam 23:13

And David was then in a hold, and the garrison of the Philistines was then in Bethlehem.

2Sam 23:14

And David longed, and said, Oh that one would give me a drink of the water of the well of Bethlehem, which is by the gate!

2Sam 23:15

And the three mighty men break through the host of the Philistines, and drew water out of the well of Bethlehem, that was by the gate, and took it, and brought it to David: nevertheless, he would not drink thereof but poured it out unto the LORD.

2Sam 23:16

And he said, Be it far from me, O LORD, that I should do this: is not this the blood of the men that went in jeopardy of their lives? therefore he would not drink it. These things did these three mighty men.

2Sam 23:17

We read of these accounts of King David's mighty men; they were determined to win the victory at any cost, even unto death.

To commit is to have a pledge or a promise. A made-up mind. Just as the football team is committed to winning, we must be committed to winning too.

Let us look at four commitments; one Mission, two Memberships, three Maturities, and three Ministries; four is Back to Missions. It is like a baseball diamond.

There is home, first, second, and third and back home. Between these bases is the track that the player runs on four tracks; on these four tracks, we can see four things to get closer to the Lord. Track one is knowing Christ, track two is growing in Christ, track three is serving Christ, and track four is sharing Christ. Now let us put this into play and see how well we can commit ourselves to Jesus Christ. Romans 10:14-15,

How then shall they call on him in whom they have not believed? and how shall they believe in him of whom they have not heard? and how shall they hear without a preacher?

Rom 10:14

And how shall they preach, except they be sent? As it is written, How beautiful are the feet of them that preach the gospel of peace, and bring glad tidings of good things!

Rom 10:15

It all begins at home base when a man on a mission tells us about Jesus. As a sinner, we accept Jesus as our Lord and Savior. Romans 10 tells us this,

But what saith it? The word is nigh thee, even in thy mouth, and in thy heart: that is, the word of faith, which we preach;

Rom 10:8

That if thou shalt confess with thy mouth the Lord Jesus, and shalt believe in thine heart that God hath raised him from the dead, thou shalt be saved.

Rom 10:9

For with the heart, man believeth unto righteousness, and with the mouth, confession is made unto salvation.

Rom 10:10

For the scripture saith, Whosoever, believeth on him shall not be ashamed.

Rom 10:11

For there is no difference between the Jew and the Greek: for the same Lord over all is rich unto all that call upon him.

Rom 10:12

For whosoever shall call upon the name of the Lord shall be saved.

Rom 10:13

So, the ball is hit, and the game is on, and we run the first track Knowing Jesus. Running to first base, we find ourselves in a membership with the church. Looking at 1 Corinthians 16:13- 16, 13

Watch ye, stand fast in the faith, quit you like men, be strong.

Let all your things be done with charity.

1Co 16:14

I beseech you, brethren, (ye know the house of Stephanas, that it is the firstfruits of Achaia, and that they have addicted themselves to the ministry of the saints,)

1Co 16:15

That ye submit yourselves unto such, and to every one that helpeth with us, and laboureth.

1Co 16:16

When we addict ourselves to the gospel, we begin to have a membership with the Saints. All Christians need to belong to a Bible-believing Spirit-filled church so they can grow.

By having a membership in Christ, we can go on to the second base of maturity and the track of growing in Christ.

We all are a member of the body of Christ looking at 1 Corinthians 12:12-31,

For as the body is one, and hath many members, and all the members of that one body, being many, are one body: so also, is Christ.

1Co 12:12

For by one Spirit are we all baptized into one body, whether we be Jews or Gentiles, whether we be bond or free; and have been all made to drink into one spirit.

1Co 12:13

For the body is not one member, but many.

1Co 12:14

If the foot shall say, Because I am not the hand, I am not of the body; is it therefore not of the body?

1Co 12:15

And if the ear shall say, Because I am not the eye, I am not of the

body; is it therefore not of the body?

1Co 12:16

If the whole body were an eye, where were the hearing? If the whole were hearing, where were the smelling?

1Co 12:17

But now hath God set the members every one of them in the body, as it hath pleased him.

1Co 12:18

And if they were all one member, where were the body?

1Co 12:19

But now are they many members, yet but one body.

1Co 12:20

And the eye cannot say unto the hand, I have no need of thee: nor again the head to the feet, I have no need of you.

1Co 12:21

Nay, much more those members of the body, which seem to be more feeble, are necessary:

1Co 12:22

And those members of the body, which we think to be less honourable, upon these we bestow more abundant honour; and our uncomely parts have more abundant comeliness.

1Co 12:23

For our comely parts have no need: but God hath tempered the body together, having given more abundant honour to that part which lacked:

1Co 12:24

That there should be no schism in the body; but that the members should have the same care one for another.

1Co 12:25

And whether one member suffers, all the members suffer with it, or one member be honoured, all the members rejoice with it.

1Co 12:26

Now ye are the body of Christ, and members in particular.

1Co 12:27

And God hath set some in the church, first apostles, secondarily prophets, thirdly teachers, after that miracles, then gifts of healing, help, governments, diversities of tongues.

1Co 12:28

Are all apostles? Are all prophets? Are all teachers? are all workers of miracles?

1Co 12:29

Have all the gifts of healing? do all speak with tongues? do all interpret?

1Co 12:30

But covet earnestly the best gifts: and yet shew I unto you a more excellent way.

1Co 12:31

By committing ourselves to Christ and the Church, we will continue to grow to maturity.

The body of Christ has many members but one body. It is in Baptismal that we become one with Christ through the spirit.

And he said unto them, Go ye into all the world, and preach the gospel to every creature.

Mark 16:15

He that believeth and is baptized shall be saved; but he that believeth not shall be damned.

Mark 16:16

And these signs shall follow them that believe; In my name shall they cast out devils; they shall speak with new tongues;

Mark 16:17

They shall take up serpents; and if they drink any deadly thing, it shall not hurt them; they shall lay hands on the sick, and they shall recover.

Mark 16:18

As a body, we have a mission; as an individual, we have a mission; we learn about Jesus together. We grow in Christ together and mature in Christ together. As we mature, we learn to serve Christ together then we learn to commit to a ministry. What are the ministries? Let us look at the Scriptures,

So we, being many, are one body in Christ, and every member one of another.

Romans 12:5

Having then gifts differing according to the grace that is given to us, whether prophecy, let us prophesy according to the the proportion of faith;

Rom 12:6

Or ministry, let us wait on our ministering: or he that teacheth, on teaching;

Rom 12:7

Or he that exhorteth, on exhortation: he that giveth, let him do it with simplicity; he that ruleth, with diligence; he that sheweth mercy, with cheerfulness.

Rom 12:8

Let love be without dissimulation. Abhor that which is evil; cleave to that which is good.

Rom 12:9

Be kindly affectioned one to another with brotherly love; in honour preferring one another;

Rom 12:10

Not slothful in business; fervent in spirit; serving the Lord;

Rom 12:11

Rejoicing in hope; patient in tribulation; continuing instant in prayer;

Rom 12:12

Distributing to the necessity of saints; given to hospitality.

Rom 12:13

Bless them which persecute you: bless, and curse not.

Rom 12:14

Rejoice with them that do rejoice, and weep with them that weep.

Rom 12:15

Be of the same mind one toward another. Mind not high things, but condescend to men of low estate. Be not wise in your own conceits.

Rom 12:16

Be ready to give of yourself anytime, like being an altar worker in the church. That is a calling; it is to be ready to give of yourself till there is victory, be a prayer warrior.

Now ye are the body of Christ and members in particular.

1Corinthians 12:27

And God hath set some in the church, first apostles, secondarily prophets, thirdly teachers, after that miracles, then gifts of healings, helps, governments, diversities of tongues.

1Co 12:28

Are all apostles? Are all prophets? Are all teachers? are all workers of miracles?

1Co 12:29

Have all the gifts of healing? do all speak with tongues? do all interpret?

1Co 12:30

But covet earnestly the best gifts: and yet shew I unto you a more excellent way.

1Co 12:31

As we see there are many callings in the ministry that we can do. And he gave some, apostles; and some, prophets; and some, evangelists; and some, pastors and teachers;

Eph 4:11

For the perfecting of the saints, for the work of the ministry, for the edifying of the body of Christ:

Eph 4:12

Till we all come in the unity of the faith, and of the knowledge of the Son of God, unto a perfect man, unto the measure of the stature of the fulness of Christ:

Eph 4:13

That we henceforth be no more children, tossed to and fro, and carried about with every wind of doctrine, by the sleight of men, and cunning craftiness, whereby they lie in wait to deceive;

Eph 4:14

But speaking the truth in love may grow up into him in all things, which is the head, even Christ:

Eph 4:15

From whom the whole body fitly joined together and compacted by that which every joint supplieth, according to the effectual working in the measure of every part, maketh increase of the body unto the edifying of itself in love

Eph 4:16

After we leave the third base of ministry, we are on our way back home on the track of sharing Christ. And we come into home base to us being a mission worker our self.

In this illustration of a baseball diamond, we can learn to grow and to commit ourselves to Jesus Christ. By committing, we can attack the enemy.

Chapter 15 Attack with Zeal, Knowledge, and Wisdom

What is zeal? Zeal means to have great energy for a cause. We, as Christians, need a great desire to live for Jesus. We need to be zealous and have a great burning desire to live for God. Let us look at King Jehu in the book of 2 King 10:16,

And he said, Come with me, and see my zeal for the LORD. So, they made him ride in his chariot.

Reading the whole of Chapter 10, we will find that Jehu had the desire to kill all the prophets of Baal. In which, with the zeal of God, he did so. God gave Jehu a promise that if he would walk upright before The Lord, he would bless him even to the fourth generation. But Jehu did not walk in the ways of the Lord.

There is one man who had a zeal for God. St. Paul not only had great zeal, but he also had knowledge and wisdom. Looking at the account of Paul before King Agrippa and the fetus is an example of his zeal.

Whereupon as I went to Damascus with authority and commission from the chief priests,

Act 26:12

At midday, O king, I saw in the way a light from heaven, above the brightness of the sun, shining round about me and them which journeyed with me.

Act 26:13

And when we were all fallen to the earth, I heard a voice speaking unto me, and saying in the Hebrew tongue, Saul, Saul, why persecutest thou me? it is hard for thee to kick against the pricks.

Act 26:14

And I said, Who art thou, Lord? And he said I am Jesus whom thou persecutest.

Act 26:15

But rise, and stand upon thy feet: for I have appeared unto thee for this purpose, to make thee a minister and a witness both of these things which thou hast seen and of those things in the which I will appear unto thee;

Act 26:16

Delivering thee from the people, and from the Gentiles, unto whom now I send thee,

Act 26:17

To open their eyes, and to turn them from darkness to light, and from the power of Satan unto God, that they may receive forgiveness of sins, and inheritance among them which are sanctified by faith that is in me.

Act 26:18

Whereupon, O king Agrippa, I was not disobedient unto the heavenly vision:

Act 26:19

But shewed first unto them of Damascus, and at Jerusalem, and throughout all the coasts of Judaea, and then to the Gentiles, that they should repent and turn to God, and do works meet for repentance.

Act 26:20

For these causes the Jews caught me in the temple, and went about to kill me.

Act 26:21

Having therefore obtained the help of God, I continue unto this day, witnessing both to small and great, saying none other things than those which the prophets and Moses did say should come:

Act 26:22

That Christ should suffer, and that he should be the first that should rise from the dead, and should shew light unto the people, and to the Gentiles.

Act 26:23

And as he thus spake for himself, Festus said with a loud voice, Paul, thou art beside thyself; much learning doth make thee mad.

Act 26:24

But he said, I am not mad, most noble Festus; but speak forth the words of truth and soberness.

Act 26:25

For the king knoweth of these things, before whom also I speak freely: for I am persuaded that none of these things are hidden from him; for this thing was not done in a corner.

Act 26:26

King Agrippa, believest thou the prophets? I know that thou believest.

Act 26:27

Then Agrippa said unto Paul, Almost, thou persuadest me to be a Christian.

Act 26:28

And Paul said I would to God, that not only thou, but also all that hear me this day, were both almost, and altogether such as I am, except for these bonds.

Act 26:29

Saul started with a zeal to do away with all the Christians he could. His greatest desire was to persecute and put to death every Christian he found, but on his way to Damascus, Jesus met him; we read where Saul was saved; later on, Saul's name was changed to Paul.

Paul's zeal changed from his own desire or zeal to live for Jesus and to spread His word of salvation.

Fetus said, Paul, thou art beside thyself; much learning doth make thee mad Paul's zeal was greater than what Fetus had to say.

Our zeal needs to be for Jesus. We need a burning desire to live for the Lord and to spread His word with knowledge and wisdom.

What is knowledge? Is a range of information, awareness, understanding, and enlightenment. Jesus said this;

But he that knew not, and did commit things worthy of stripes, shall be beaten with few stripes. For unto whomsoever much is given, of him shall be much required: and to whom men have committed much, of him, they will ask the more.

Luke 12:48

The more we learn, the more is required of us. We never stop learning. We gain Knowledge every day. Knowledge has always been from the beginning. Looking at Genesis 2:9

And out of the ground made the LORD God to grow every tree that is pleasant to the sight, and good for food; the tree of life also in the midst of the garden, and the tree of knowledge of good and evil.

Gen 2:9

So knowledge can be good, or it can be evil. In the scripture above, it is good and evil.

What about knowing to do good what does that produce? When we know it is a sin, and we reject that sin, and we do not sin, then it becomes wisdom.

The fear of the LORD is the beginning of knowledge: but fools despise wisdom and instruction.

Proverbs 1:7

We must have these three to Attack the enemy. The more we learn, the more we know, and the more we can defeat the enemy.

Having the knowledge to use the zeal is using wisdom to overcome sin. The more we learn of the Word of God, the closer we get to Jesus and can overcome Satan.

Nay, in all these things, we are more than conquerors through him that loved us.

Rom 8:37

Chapter 16 Attacking with Love

Love can and will cover all areas of a person's life. There is love between a husband and wife, there is love between parents and children, there is love between a person and their hobbies and there is love between a person and their master. Who is your master? Jesus said this,

No man can serve two masters: for either he will hate the one, and love the other; or else he will hold to the one, and despise the other. Ye cannot serve God and mammon.

Matthew 6:24

Let us look at one love that will surpass all other love, Agape love is the highest form of love, the love between God and man. One scripture can explain God's love for man.

For God so loved the world, that he gave his only begotten Son, that whosoever believeth in him should not perish, but have everlasting life.

John 3:16

This scripture tells of how God loved the whole world that he gave his only son Jesus Christ to shed his blood for all of mankind.

I believe that Paul said this about love in the book of 1

Corinthians 13,

Though I speak with the tongues of men and of angels and have not charity, I am become as sounding brass, or a tinkling cymbal.

1Co 13:1

And though I have the gift of prophecy, and understand all mysteries and all knowledge; and though I have all faith, so that I could remove mountains, and have not charity, I am nothing.

1Co 13:2

And though I bestow all my goods to feed the poor, and though I give my body to be burned, and have not charity, it profiteth me nothing.

1Co 13:3

Charity suffereth long, and is kind; charity envieth not; charity vaunteth not itself, is not puffed up,

1Co 13:4

Doth not behave itself unseemly, seeketh not her own, is not easily provoked, thinketh no evil;

1Co 13:5

Rejoiceth not in iniquity, but rejoiceth in the truth;

1Co 13:6

Beareth all things, believeth all things, hopeth all things, endureth all things.

1Co 13:7

Charity never faileth: but whether there be prophecies, they shall fail; whether there be tongues, they shall cease; whether there be knowledge, it shall vanish away.

1Co 13:8

For we know in part, and we prophesy in part.

1Co 13:9

But when that which is perfect is come, then that which is in part shall be done away.

1Co 13:10

When I was a child, I spake as a child, I understood as a child, I thought as a child: but when I became a man, I put away childish things.

1Co 13:11

For now, we see through a glass, darkly; but then face to face: now I know in part; but then shall I know even as also I am known.

1Co 13:12

And now abideth faith, hope, charity, these three; but the greatest of these is charity.

1Co 13:13

Charity is love. This chapter tells us to give off ourselves to one another. I believe Paul sums it all up in verse 13, faith, hope, charity; but the greatest is charity or meaning love. When we have love we will know how to forgive.

What does Jesus say about love? Let us look at what The Lord said about love.

Ye have heard that it hath been said, Thou shalt love thy neighbour and hate thine enemy.

Mat 5:43

But I say unto you, Love your enemies, bless them that curse you, do good to them that hate you, and pray for them which despitefully use you, and persecute you;

Mat 5:44

That ye may be the children of your Father which is in heaven: for he maketh his sun to rise on the evil and on the good, and sendeth rain on the just and on the unjust.

Mat 5:45

For if ye love them which love you, what reward have ye? do not even the publicans the same?

Mat 5:46

And if ye salute your brethren only, what do ye more than others? do not even the publicans so?

Mat 5:47

Be ye therefore perfect, even as your Father which is in heaven is perfect.

Mat 5:48

Here in the book of Matthew, Jesus is speaking of a love that reaches Father down than we can reach up. When we love with the agape love we will even pray for our enemies. Jesus said this, in the book John,

This is my commandment, That ye love one another, as I have loved you.

Joh 15:12

Greater love hath no man than this, that a man lay down his life for his friends.

Joh 15:13

Ye are my friends, if ye do whatsoever I command you.

Joh 15:14

Henceforth I call you not servants; for the servant knoweth not what his lord doeth: but I have called you friends;for all things that I have heard of my Father, I have made known unto you.

Joh 15:15

Ye have not chosen me, but I have chosen you, and ordained you, that ye should go and bring forth fruit, and that your fruit should remain: that whatsoever ye shall ask of the Father in my name, he may give it to you.

Joh 15:16

These things I command you, that ye love one another.

Joh 15:17

If the world hate you, ye know that it hated me before it hated you.

Joh 15:18

If ye were of the world, the world would love his own: but because ye are not of the world, but I have chosen you out of the world, therefore the world hateth you.

Joh 15:19

Remember the word that I said unto you, The servant is not greater than his lord. If they have persecuted me, they will also persecute you; if they have kept my saying, they will keep yours also.

Joh 15:20

But all these things will they do unto you for my name's sake, because they know not him that sent me.

Joh 15:21

We as Brother and Sisters in Jesus Christ are to love one another. By having that agape love for one another we will attack Satan with a good blow to the eye. We the Church must have love otherwise we have nothing. We must give up ourselves to help one another. When we show love, we will build up our faith in the Lord. When we have the fruit of love we will have a work of faith. Faith without work is dead. James tells us this, concerning faith and works.

What doth it profit, my brethren, though a man say he hath faith, and have not works? can faith save him?

Jas 2:14

If a brother or sister be naked, and destitute of daily food,

Jas 2:15

And one of you say unto them, Depart in peace, be ye warmed and filled; notwithstanding ye give them not those things which are needful to the body; what doth it profit?

Jas 2:16

Even so, faith, if it hath not worked, is dead, being alone.

Jas 2:17

Yea, a man may say, Thou hast faith, and I have works: shew me thy faith without thy works, and I will shew thee my faith by my works.

Jas 2:18

Thou believest that there is one God; thou doest well: the devils also believe, and tremble.

Jas 2:19

But wilt thou know, O vain man, that faith without works is dead?

Jas 2:20

So, we read and learn that these two go hand in hand like a marriage.

A marriage must have love, without the love between spouses, the marriage becomes dead for there is nothing left there. We must have faith and works. St. John goes on and tells us this in 1 John 2:7-17

Brethren, I write no new commandment unto you, but an old commandment which ye had from the beginning. The old commandment is the word which ye have heard from the beginning.

1Jn 2:7

Again, a new commandment I write unto you, which thing is true in him and in you: because the darkness is past, and the true light now shineth.

1Jn 2:8

He that saith he is in the light, and hateth his brother, is in darkness even until now.

1Jn 2:9

He that loveth his brother abideth in the light, and there is none occasion of stumbling in him.

1Jn 2:10

But he that hateth his brother is in darkness, and walketh in darkness, and knoweth not whither he goeth, because that darkness hath blinded his eyes.

1Jn 2:11

I write unto you, little children because your sins are forgiven you for his name's sake.

1Jn 2:12

I write unto you, fathers because ye have known him that is from the beginning. I write unto you, young men because ye have overcome the wicked one. I write unto you, little children because ye have known the Father.

1Jn 2:13

I have written unto you, fathers, because ye have known him that is from the beginning. I have written unto you, young men, because ye are strong, and the word of God abideth in you and ye have overcome the wicked one.

1Jn 2:14

Love is not the world, nor the things that are in the world. If any man loves the world, the love of the Father is not in him.

1Jn 2:15

For all that is in the world, the lust of the flesh, and the lust of the eyes, and the pride of life, is not of the Father but is of the world.

1Jn 2:16

And the world passeth away, and the lust thereof: but he that doeth the will of God abideth forever.

1Jn 2:17

Yes, Christians can attack with love, we must attack with an agape love, not the love of the world. The love of this world will fade away but, the love that God has for man will last forever. The agape love of God.

Chapter 17 Attacking with Faith and Works

We talked a little in the last chapter about it. I felt like we needed to go over more on faith and works. Let us revisit James 2 but will look at more verses.

What doth it profit, my brethren, though a man say he hath faith, and have not works? can faith save him?

Jas 2:14

If a brother or sister be naked, and destitute of daily food,

Jas 2:15

And one of you say unto them, Depart in peace, be ye warmed and filled; notwithstanding ye give them, not those things which are needful to the body; what doth it profit?

Jas 2:16

Even so, faith, if it hath not works, is dead, being alone.

Jas 2:17

Yea, a man may say, Thou hast faith, and I have works: shew me thy faith without thy works, and I will shew thee my faith by my works.

Jas 2:18

Thou believest that there is one God; thou doest well: the devils also believe, and tremble.

Jas 2:19

But wilt thou know, O vain man, that faith without works is dead?

Jas 2:20

Was not Abraham our father justified by works, when he had offered Isaac his son upon the altar?

Jas 2:21

Seest thou how faith wrought with his works, and by works was faith made perfect?

Jas 2:22

And the scripture was fulfilled which saith, Abraham believed God, and it was imputed unto him for righteousness: and he was called the Friend of God.

Jas 2:23

Ye see then how that by works a man is justified, and not by faith only.

Jas 2:24

Likewise, also was not Rahab the harlot justified by works, when she had received the messengers, and had sent them out another way?

Jas 2:25

For as the body without the spirit is dead, so faith without works is dead also.

Jas 2:26

We have spoken earlier of how a marriage must have love to survive, same with faith and works, they must have each other to survive. Let us look these two individuals for a better understanding of the word of God. We spoke of faith earlier, we will speak of faith a little more. Abraham had a son by the name of Isaac; in the book of Genesis, chapter 22, Abraham is put to the test by the Lord. He was told to sacrifice his only son to the Lord. So, he took his son to the place, Isaac asked his father where the sacrifice was. Abraham replied that God would provide, and God did provide. Abraham acted on pure faith that some way somehow God would keep his promise to him.

Abraham's faith was and is still whole today. So, what is our faith? A better question is. What is your faith? A lot of people will answer you, denomination is my faith. Faith has nothing to do with denomination. Faith is in God the Father, Jesus the Son, and the Holy Ghost. There is but one way to heaven, and the only way to heaven is in Jesus Christ, the son of God. Jesus is (the way) not a way. Jesus said this,

Jesus saith unto him, I am the way, the truth, and the life: no man cometh unto the Father, but by me.

John 14:6

Jesus is the only way to the Father. Let us look at Romans 10:8-17,

But what saith it? The word is nigh thee, even in thy mouth, and in thy heart: that is, the word of faith, which we preach;

Rom 10:8

That if thou shalt confess with thy mouth the Lord Jesus, and shalt believe in thine heart that God hath raised him from the dead, thou shalt be saved.

Rom 10:9

For with the heart man believeth unto righteousness; and with the mouth confession is made unto salvation.

Rom 10:10

For the scripture saith, Whosoever, believeth on him shall not be ashamed.

Rom 10:11

For there is no difference between the Jew and the Greek: for the same Lord over all is rich unto all that call upon him.

Rom 10:12

For whosoever shall call upon the name of the Lord shall be saved.

Rom 10:13

How then shall they call on him in whom they have not believed? and how shall they believe in him of whom they have not heard? and how shall they hear without a preacher?

Rom 10:14

And how shall they preach, except they be sent? as it is written,How beautiful are the feet of them that preach the gospel of peace, and

bring glad tidings of good things!

Rom 10:15

But they have not all obeyed the gospel. For Esaias saith, Lord, who hath believed our report?

Rom 10:16

So, then faith cometh by hearing, and hearing by the word of God.

Rom 10:17

I believe this is plain. We call on the name of the Lord Jesus Christ; we shall be saved. What did Jesus say?

And he said unto them, Go ye into all the world, and preach the gospel to every creature.

Mark 16:15

He that believeth and is baptized shall be saved; but he that believeth not shall be damned.

Mark 16:16

And these signs shall follow them that believe; In my name shall they cast out devils; they shall speak with new tongues;

Mark 16:17

They shall take up serpents; and if they drink any deadly thing, it shall not hurt them; they shall lay hands on the sick, and they shall recover.

Mark16:18 Jesus said, He that believeth and is baptized shall be saved. We must believe first; if we do not believe and we go under the water, we will come up a wet sinner and not be saved. We must believe first. By believing, we plant a seed, a seed of faith in the Lord Jesus Christ. So, what about works? What is or works? Remember, faith without works is dead. Jesus said this in Matthew 25:31- 46,

When the Son of man shall come in his glory, and all the holy angels with him, then shall he sit upon the throne of his glory:

Mark16:18

And before him shall be gathered all nations: and he shall separate them one from another, as a shepherd divideth his sheep from the goats:

Mat 25:32

And he shall set the sheep on his right hand, but the goats on the left.

Mat 25:33

Then shall the King say unto them on his right hand, Come, ye blessed of my Father, inherit the kingdom prepared for you from the foundation of the world:

Mat 25:34

For I was an hungered, and ye gave me meat: I was thirsty, and ye gave me drink: I was a stranger, and ye took me in:

Mat 25:35

Naked, and ye clothed me: I was sick, and ye visited me: I was in prison, and ye came unto me.

Mat 25:36

hen shall the righteous answer him, saying, Lord, when saw we thee an hungered, and fed thee? or thirsty, and gave thee drink?

Mat 25:37

When saw we thee a stranger, and took thee in? or naked, and clothed thee?

Mat 25:38

Or when saw we thee sick or in prison, and came unto thee?

Mat 25:39

And the King shall answer and say unto them, Verily I say unto you, Inasmuch as ye have done it unto one of the least of these my brethren, ye have done it unto me.

Mat 25:40

Then shall he say also unto them on the left hand, Depart from me, ye cursed, into everlasting fire, prepared for the devil and his angels:

Mat 25:41

For I was an hungered, and ye gave me no meat: I was thirsty, and ye gave me no drink:

Mat 25:42

I was a stranger, and ye took me not in: naked, and ye clothed me not: sick, and in prison, and ye visited me not.

Mat 25:43

Then shall they also answer him, saying, Lord, when saw we thee an hungered, or athirst, or a stranger, or naked, or sick, or in prison, and did not minister unto thee?

Mat 25:44

Then shall he answer them, saying, Verily I say unto you, Inasmuch as ye did it not to one of the least of these, ye did it not to me.

Mat 25:45

And these shall go away into everlasting punishment: but the righteous into life eternal.

Mat 25:46

When we feed the hungry and give them to drink in this case, I believe it is water to give a stranger shelter, clothe the naked, visit the sick, and take the word of faith to those who are in prison. When we open up our bowls of mercy and do the works of the Lord, then in return, we will produce fruit. What is our fruit? Galatians 5:22-26 tells us this,

But the fruit of the Spirit is love, joy, peace, longsuffering, gentleness, goodness, faith,

Gal 5:22

Meekness, temperance: against such there is no law.

Gal 5:23

And they that are Christ's have crucified the flesh with the affections

and lusts.

Gal 5:24

If we live in the Spirit, let us also walk in the Spirit.

Gal 5:25

Let us not be desirous of vain glory, provoking one another, envying one another.

Gal 5:26

These are the fruits that we will bear. So, where are your fruits? What are your fruits? Colossians 3:12-17 tells us,

Put on, therefore, as the elect of God, holy and beloved, bowels of mercies, kindness, humbleness of mind, meekness, longsuffering;

Col 3:12

Forbearing one another, and forgiving one another, if any man have a quarrel against any: even as Christ forgave you, so also do ye.

Col 3:13

And above all these things put on charity, which is the bond of perfectness.

Col 3:14

And let the peace of God rule in your hearts, to the which also ye are called in one body; and be ye thankful.

Col 3:15

Let the word of Christ dwell in you richly in all wisdom; teaching and admonishing one another in psalms and hymns and spiritual songs, singing with grace in your hearts to the Lord.

Col 3:16

And whatsoever ye do in word or deed, do all in the name of the Lord Jesus, giving thanks to God and the Father by him.

Col 3:17

When we put Faith and works together and bind them with the love of

God, we will be able to attack Satan with the fullness of the Word of God. We must attack Satan with all that God has to offer. It is when we turn it all over to God that we can win this spiritual battle.

Chapter 18 There Is Victory

O sing unto the LORD a new song; for he hath done marvellous things: his right hand, and his holy arm, hath gotten him the victory.

Psalms 98:1 A Psalm.

The LORD hath made known his salvation: his righteousness hath he openly shewed in the sight of the heathen.

Psa 98:2

He hath remembered his mercy and his truth toward the house of Israel: all the ends of the earth have seen the salvation of our God.

Psa 98:3

Make a joyful noise unto the LORD, all the earth: make a loud noise, and rejoice, and sing praise.

Psa 98:4

Sing unto the LORD with the harp; with the harp, and the voice of a psalm.

Psa 98:5

With trumpets and sound of cornet make a joyful noise before the LORD, the King.

Psa 98:6

Let the sea roar and the fulness thereof; the world, and they that dwell therein.

Psa 98:7

Let the floods clap their hands: let the hills be joyful together.

Psa 98:8

Before the LORD; for he cometh to judge the earth: with righteousness shall he judge the world, and the people with equity.

Psa 98:9

King David said, to sing a new song, for by the hand of God and his arm, God brought victory.

We all have had our victories and our losses. In this chapter, we will discuss how we got the victory and battles that we all have lost but went back and won, thus winning the victory. We have had our red sea of discouragements but, in the end, there was victory brought by the arm of God. Turn with me to the book of Exodus, chapter 14. Israel is being led out of Egypt, out of the hand of Pharaoh. Pharaoh starts after Israel and then they come to the Bank of the Red Sea. Oh, did the children of Israel begin to complain? It amazes me how Christians complain today, yet God has his mercy and delivers his people. Let us look at what truly happened on that day. Not what movies say that happen but what the scriptures say. Let us

pick up in Chapter 14:13-31,

And Moses said unto the people, Fear ye not, stand still, and see the salvation of the LORD, which he will shew to you to day: for the Egyptians whom ye have seen today, ye shall see them again no more forever.

Exo 14:13

The LORD shall fight for you, and ye shall hold your peace.

Exo 14:14

And the LORD said unto Moses, Wherefore, criest thou unto me? speak unto the children of Israel, that they go forward:

Exo 14:15

But lift thou up thy rod, and stretch out thine hand over the sea, and divide it: and the children of Israel shall go on dry ground through the midst of the sea.

Exo 14:16

And I, behold, I will harden the hearts of the Egyptians, and they shall follow them: and I will get me honour upon Pharaoh, and upon all his host, upon his chariots, and upon his horsemen.

Exo 14:17

And the Egyptians shall know that I am the LORD when I have gotten me honour upon Pharaoh, upon his chariots, and upon his horsemen.

Exo 14:18

And the angel of God, which went before the camp of Israel, removed and went behind them; and the pillar of the cloud went from before their face, and stood behind them:

Exo 14:19

And it came between the camp of the Egyptians and the camp of Israel, and it was a cloud and darkness to them, but it gave light by night to these: so that the one came not near the other all the night.

Exo 14:20

And Moses stretched out his hand over the sea, and the LORD caused the sea to go back by a strong east wind all that night, and made the sea dry land, and the waters were divided.

Exo 14:21

And the children of Israel went into the midst of the sea upon the dry ground: and the waters were a wall unto them on their right hand, and on their left.

Exo 14:22

And the Egyptians pursued and went in after them to the midst of the sea, even all Pharaoh's horses, his chariots, and his horsemen.

Exo 14:23

And it came to pass, that in the morning watch the LORD looked unto the host of the Egyptians through the pillar of fire and of the cloud, and troubled the host of the Egyptians,

Exo 14:24

And took off their chariot wheels, that they drave them heavily: so that the Egyptians said, Let us flee from the face of Israel; for the LORD fighteth for them against the Egyptians.

Exo 14:25

And the LORD said unto Moses, Stretch out thine hand over the sea, that the waters may come again upon the Egyptians, upon their chariots, and upon their horsemen.

Exo 14:26

And Moses stretched forth his hand over the sea, and the sea returned to his strength when the morning appeared, and the Egyptians fled against it, and the LORD overthrew the Egyptians in the midst of the sea.

Exo 14:27

And the waters returned, and covered the chariots, and the horsemen, and all the host of Pharaoh that came into the sea after them; there remained not so much as one of them.

Exo 14:28

But the children of Israel walked upon dry land in the midst of the sea, and the waters were a wall unto them on their right hand, and on their left.

Exo 14:29

Thus, the LORD saved Israel that day out of the hand of the Egyptians, and Israel saw the Egyptians dead upon the seashore.

Exo 14:30

And Israel saw that great work which the LORD did upon the Egyptians: and the people feared the LORD, and believed the LORD, and his servant Moses.

Exo 14:31

Oh, what a victory that was brought by the hand of God. Hollywood tells a lie in the movies. They say that Pharaoh stays alive and standing on the bank. Let us look and see what the Word of God has to say,

With a strong hand, and with a stretched out arm: for his mercy endureth forever.

Psa 136:12

To him which divided the Red Sea into parts: for his mercy endureth forever:

Psa 136:13

And made Israel to pass through the midst of it: for his mercy endureth forever:

Psa 136:14

But overthrew Pharaoh and his host in the Red sea: for his mercy endureth forever.

Psa 136:15

A great victory was won; Pharaoh and his armies died in the Red Sea that day. You may come up to your sea of discouragements but hold on. God will divide that sea of discouragements and you will walk into victory.

In order to have victory, we must fight. In Joshua chapter 6, God gave Israel a great victory over Jericho. The walls of that city came tumbling down. Let us look at this way, in our walk with the Lord, we come against spiritual walls. The only to see the wall to come down is to put it into the hands of the living God.

That is what happened to Joshua looking at these scriptures Joshua 5:13-15,

And it came to pass, when Joshua was by Jericho, that he lifted up his eyes and looked, and, behold, there stood a man over against him with his sword drawn in his hand: and Joshua went unto him, and said unto him, Art thou for us, or for our adversaries?

Jos 5:13

And he said, Nay; but as captain of the host of the LORD am I now come. And Joshua fell on his face to the earth, and did worship, and said unto him, What saith my lord unto his servant?

Jos 5:14

And the captain of the LORD'S host said unto Joshua, Loose thy shoe from off thy foot; for the place whereon thou standest is holy. And

Joshua did so.

Jos 5:15

Many times, I have come against things in my walk with the Lord and let me say this I have always found that God will send his heavenly host of angels to overcome; there is victory when the walls of the enemy come down. Israel sinned. A sin that cost a man's life and his family's life. Sin has a repercussion like a still lake when a rock is thrown in and it causes a wave all the way to the banks. In Joshua 7, there was a man by the name of Achan; he had stolen an accursed thing and hidden it. There was sin in the camp. Israel went to battle at AI and lost the battle at AI. Joshua went to prayer before the Lord and God revealed to Joshua that there was sin in the camp.

Achan was found and he and his family were put to death. Israel went back to battle and won the victory.

When there is sin in the camp, there will never be a victory. All sin must come under the blood of Jesus Christ and complete repentance; then, you will see the victory.

We no longer live under the law of Moses but we live under grace. Having grace does not give us the license to sin, but grace frees us from sin.

What shall we say then? Shall we continue in sin, that grace may abound?

Rom 6:1

God forbid. How shall we, that are dead to sin, live any longer therein?

Rom 6:2

Know ye not, that so many of us as were baptized into Jesus Christ were baptized into his death?

Rom 6:3

Therefore, we are buried with him by baptism into death: that like as Christ was raised up from the dead by the glory of the Father, even so, we also should walk in newness of life.

Rom 6:4

For if we have been planted together in the likeness of his death, we shall be also in the likeness of his resurrection:

Rom 6:5

Knowing this, that our old man is crucified with him, that the body of sin might be destroyed, that henceforth we should not serve sin.

Rom 6:6

For he that is dead is freed from sin.

Rom 6:7

Now if we be dead with Christ, we believe that we shall also live with him:

Rom 6:8

Knowing that Christ being raised from the dead dieth no more; death hath no more dominion over him.

Rom 6:9

For in that he died, he died unto sin once: but in that he liveth, he liveth unto God.

Rom 6:10

Likewise reckon ye also yourselves to be dead indeed unto sin, but alive unto God through Jesus Christ our Lord.

Rom 6:11

Let not sin therefore reign in your mortal body, that ye should obey it in the lusts thereof.

Rom 6:12

Neither yield ye your members as instruments of unrighteousness unto sin: but yield yourselves unto God, as those that are alive from the dead, and your members as instruments of righteousness unto God.

Rom 6:13

For sin shall not have dominion over you: for ye are not under the law, but under grace.

Rom 6:14

What then? shall we sin, because we are not under the law, but under grace? God forbid.

Rom 6:15

Know ye not, that to whom ye yield yourselves servants to obey, his servants ye are to whom ye obey; whether of sin unto death, or of obedience unto righteousness?

Rom 6:16

But God be thanked, that ye were the servants of sin, but ye have obeyed from the heart that form of doctrine which was delivered you.

Rom 6:17

Being then made free from sin, ye became the servants of righteousness.

Rom 6:18

I speak after the manner of men because of the infirmity of your flesh: for as ye have yielded your members servants to uncleanness and to iniquity unto iniquity; even so now yield your members servants to righteousness unto holiness.

Rom 6:19

For when ye were the servants of sin, ye were free from righteousness.

Rom 6:20

What fruit had ye then in those things whereof ye are now ashamed? for the end of those things is death.

Rom 6:21

But now being made free from sin, and become servants to God, ye have your fruit unto holiness, and the end everlasting life.

Rom 6:22

For the wages of sin is death, but the gift of God is eternal life through Jesus Christ our Lord.

Rom 6:23

Living under grace we become alive in Christ Jesus; thus, we have victory over sin. Paul explains it in 1 Corinthians,

Behold, I shew you a mystery; We shall not all sleep, but we shall all be changed,

1Co 15:51

In a moment, in the twinkling of an eye, at the last trump: for the trumpet shall sound, and the dead shall be raised incorruptible, and we shall be changed.

1Co 15:52

For this corruptible must put on incorruption, and this mortal must put on immortality.

1Co 15:53

So, when this corruptible shall have put on incorruption, and this mortal shall have put on immortality, then shall be brought to pass the saying that is written, Death is swallowed up in victory.

1Co 15:54

O death, where is thy sting? O grave, where is thy victory?

1Co 15:55

The sting of death is sin; and the strength of sin is the law.

1Co 15:56

But thanks be to God, which giveth us the victory through our Lord Jesus Christ.

1Co 15:57

Therefore, my beloved brethren, be ye steadfast, unmoveable, always abounding in the work of the Lord, forasmuch as ye know that your

labour is not in vain in the Lord.

1Co 15:58

So, under grace, we will live eternally; Paul tells us in verse 58 to always keep abounding. In other words, keep growing in the work of the Lord. But what if we sin? Is there forgiveness? Yes. John tells us this,

My little children, these things write I unto you, that ye sin not. And if any man sin, we have an advocate with the Father, Jesus Christ the righteous:

1Jn 2:1

And he is the propitiation for our sins: and not for ours only, but also for the sins of the whole world.

1Jn 2:2

You can be saved for 50 years or 1 year, you will fall and at times, you will commit sin; that is why we have an advocate with the Father, Jesus Christ. In closing this chapter, let us look at three men who went through the flame.

Nebuchadnezzar the king made an image of gold, whose height was threescore cubits, and the breadth thereof six cubits: he set it up in the plain of Dura, in the province of Babylon.

Dan 3:1

Then Nebuchadnezzar the king sent to gather together the princes, the governors, and the captains, the judges, the treasurers, the counsellors, the sheriffs, and all the rulers of the provinces, to come to the dedication of the image which Nebuchadnezzar the king had set up.

Dan 3:2

Then the princes, the governors, and captains, the judges, the treasurers, the counsellors, the sheriffs, and all the rulers of the provinces, were gathered together unto the dedication of the image

that Nebuchadnezzar the king had set up; and they stood before the image that Nebuchadnezzar had set up.

Dan 3:3

Then a herald cried aloud, To you it is commanded, O people, nations, and languages,

Dan 3:4

That at what time ye hear the sound of the cornet, flute, harp, sackbut, psaltery, dulcimer, and all kinds of musick, ye fall down and worship the golden image that Nebuchadnezzar the king hath set up:

Dan 3:5

And whoso falleth not down and worshippeth shall the same hour be cast into the midst of a burning fiery furnace.

Dan 3:6

Therefore, at that time, when all the people heard the sound of the cornet, flute, harp, sackbut, psaltery, and all kinds of musick, all the people, the nations, and the languages, fell down and worshipped the golden image that Nebuchadnezzar the king had set up.

Dan 3:7

Wherefore at that time certain Chaldeans came near and accused the Jews.

Dan 3:8

They spake and said to the king Nebuchadnezzar, O king, live forever.

Dan 3:9

Thou, O king, hast made a decree, that every man that shall hear the sound of the cornet, flute, harp, sackbut, psaltery, and dulcimer, and all kinds of musick, shall fall down and worship the golden image:

Dan 3:10

And whoso falleth not down and worshippeth, that he should be cast into the midst of a burning fiery furnace.

Dan 3:11

There are certain Jews whom thou hast set over the affairs of the province of Babylon, Shadrach, Meshach, and Abednego; these men, O king, have not regarded thee: they serve not thy gods, nor worship the golden image which thou hast set up.

Dan 3:12

Then Nebuchadnezzar in his rage and fury commanded to bring Shadrach, Meshach, and Abednego. Then they brought these men before the king.

Dan 3:13

Nebuchadnezzar spake and said unto them, Is it true, O Shadrach, Meshach, and Abednego do not ye serve my gods, nor worship the golden image which I have set up?

Dan 3:14

Now if ye be ready that at what time ye hear the sound of the cornet, flute, harp, sackbut, psaltery, and dulcimer, and all kinds of musick, ye fall down and worship the image which I have made; well: but if ye worship not, ye shall be cast the same hour into the midst of a burning fiery furnace; and who is that God that shall deliver you out of my hands?

Dan 3:15

Shadrach, Meshach, and Abednego answered and said to the king, O Nebuchadnezzar, we are not careful to answer thee in this matter.

Dan 3:16

If it be so, our God whom we serve is able to deliver us from the burning fiery furnace, and he will deliver us out of thine hand, O king.

Dan 3:17

But if not, be it known unto thee, O king, that we will not serve thy gods, nor worship the golden image which thou hast set up.

Dan 3:18

Then was Nebuchadnezzar full of fury, and the form of his visage was changed against Shadrach, Meshach, and Abednego: therefore, he spake, and commanded that they should heat the furnace one seven times more than it was wont to be heated.

Dan 3:19

And he commanded the most mighty men that were in his army to bind Shadrach, Meshach, and Abednego, and to cast them into the burning fiery furnace.

Dan 3:20

Then these men were bound in their coats, their hosen, and their hats, and their other garments, and were cast into the midst of the burning fiery furnace.

Dan 3:21

Therefore, because the king's commandment was urgent, and the furnace exceeding hot, the flame of the fire slew those men that took up Shadrach, Meshach, and Abednego.

Dan 3:22

And these three men, Shadrach, Meshach, and Abednego, fell downbound into the midst of the burning fiery furnace.

Dan 3:23

Then Nebuchadnezzar the king was astonied, and rose up in haste, and spake, and said unto his counsellors, Did not we cast three men bound into the midst of the fire? They answered and said unto the king, True, O king.

Dan 3:24

He answered and said, Lo, I see four men loose, walking in the midst of the fire, and they have no hurt; and the form of the fourth is like the Son of God.

Dan 3:25

Then Nebuchadnezzar came near to the mouth of the burning fiery furnace, and spake, and said, Shadrach, Meshach, and Abednego, ye servants of the most high God, come forth, and come hither. Then Shadrach, Meshach, and Abednego came forth of the midst of the fire.

Dan 3:26

And the princes, governors, and captains, and the king's counsellors, being gathered together, saw these men, upon whose bodies the fire had no power, nor was a hair of their head singed, neither were their coats changed, nor the smell of fire had passed on them.

Dan 3:27

Then Nebuchadnezzar spake, and said, Blessed be the God of Shadrach, Meshach, and Abednego, who hath sent his angel, and delivered his servants that trusted in him, and have changed the king's word, and yielded their bodies, that they might not serve nor worship any god, except their own God.

Dan 3:28

Therefore, I make a decree, That every people, nation, and language, which speak anything amiss against the God of Shadrach, Meshach, and Abednego, shall be cut in pieces, and their houses shall be made a dunghill: because there is no other God that can deliver after this sort.

Dan 3:29

Then the king promoted Shadrach, Meshach, and Abednego, in the province of Babylon.

Dan 3:30

Brother and Sister, you do not have to walk in defeat. There is a victory for the Christian.

Chapter 19 Closing

Someone told me, Sam, you write like you are preaching; well in a way, yes, I am. I want to get the message of Jesus Christ across to a lost and dying world.

I want people to know there is hope in Jesus; there is help at the cross. There is victory in an empty tomb. There is a new world coming and Jesus is the King of kings and Lord of lords; His kingdom is being prepared.

We have talked about attacking the enemy, lust, witchcraft, gossip, excuses, falsehood, a carnal mind, and sin.

In closing, I want to remind us that Jesus is coming back after a church that is ready to meet the Lord. A church that is saved, sanctified, and Holy Ghost-filled. I was attending a revival in Oklahoma and the judgment of God fell on that church, and a call of repentance went forth. By and by, the truth came out, the pastor was having an affair with another woman in the church. Oh, did the pastor try and repent? Yes, he tried, but the damage was already done, and in the end, his wife left him and the church closed its doors and in time, the pastor died. Only God is the judge, not man. Matthew 7:21-23 tells us this,

Not everyone that saith unto me, Lord, Lord, shall enter into the kingdom of heaven; but he that doeth the will of my Father which is in heaven.

Mat 7:21

Many will say to me in that day, Lord, Lord, have we not prophesied in thy name? and in thy name have cast out devils? and in thy name done many wonderful works?

Mat 7:22

And then will I profess unto them, I never knew you: depart from me, ye that work iniquity.

Mat 7:23

Many are spreading the Word of God but, how are they living? Only God is the judge.

We can obtain victory only by sustaining sin and putting Jesus first.

I went to someone's house and this person said, Sam, I quit smoking. I asked why. They replied because I did not want to go to hell. I asked the same thing, why? The reply was I don't want to go to hell. I asked again, why? Then it dawned on them, and the reply was because Jesus asked me to and I love Jesus more than a cigarette. We must love Jesus with all that we have. Look what Jesus said in Matthew 22:34-40,

But when the Pharisees had heard that he had put the Sadducees to silence, they were gathered together.

Mat 22:34

Then one of them, which was a lawyer, asked him a question, tempting him, and saying,

Mat 22:35

Master, which is the great commandment in the law?

Mat 22:36

Jesus said unto him, Thou shalt love the Lord thy God with all thy heart, and with all thy soul, and with all thy mind.

Mat 22:37

This is the first and great commandment.

Mat 22:38

And the second is like unto it, Thou shalt love thy neighbour as thyself.

Mat 22:39

On these two commandments hang all the law and the prophets.

Mat 22:40

We are to love the lord with all our heart, soul, and mind. It takes all that we have. Jesus said this was our first commandment. Let us look at the Ten Commandments Exodus 20:1-17,

And God spake all these words, saying,

Exo 20:1

I am the LORD thy God, which have brought thee out of the land of Egypt, out of the house of bondage.

Exo 20:2

Thou shalt have no other gods before me.

Exo 20:3

Thou shalt not make unto thee any graven image or any likeness of anything that is in heaven above, or that is in the earth beneath, or that is in the water under the earth:

Exo 20:4

Thou shalt not bow down thyself to them, nor serve them: for I the LORD thy God am a jealous God, visiting the iniquity of the fathers upon the children unto the third and fourth generation of them that hate me;

Exo 20:5

And shewing mercy unto thousands of them that love me, and keep my commandments.

Exo 20:6

Thou shalt not take the name of the LORD thy God in vain; for the LORD will not hold him guiltless that taketh his name in vain.

Exo 20:7

Remember the sabbath day, to keep it holy.

Exo 20:8

Six days shalt thou labour, and do all thy work:

Exo 20:9

But the seventh day is the sabbath of the LORD thy God: in it, thou shalt not do any work, thou, nor thy son, nor thy daughter, thy manservant, nor thy maidservant, nor thy cattle, nor thy stranger that is within thy gates:

Exo 20:10

For in six days the LORD made heaven and earth, the sea, and all that in them is and rested the seventh day: wherefore the LORD blessed the sabbath day, and hallowed it.

Exo 20:11

Honour thy father and thy mother: that thy days may be long upon the land which the LORD thy God giveth thee.

Exo 20:12

Thou shalt not kill.

Exo 20:13

Thou shalt not commit adultery.

Exo 20:14

Thou shalt not steal.

Exo 20:15

Thou shalt not bear false witness against thy neighbour.

Exo 20:16

Thou shalt not covet thy neighbour's house, thou shalt not covet thy neighbour's wife, nor his manservant, nor his maidservant, nor his ox, nor his ass, nor anything that is thy neighbour's.

Exo 20:17

All these commandments carry over into the New Testament. A lot of people have made the comment, that there is nothing but do's and don’ts in the Bible. They are right. A sinner has no right to sing, testify, worship, teach, preach, or hold an office in the church. Not until they get saved and born again then they can take part. Paul tells us this in 2 Corinthians 5:17-21,

Therefore, if any man be in Christ, he is a new creature: old things

are passed away; behold, all things are become new.

2Co 5:17

And all things are of God, who hath reconciled us to himself by Jesus Christ and hath given to us the ministry of reconciliation;

2Co 5:18

To wit, that God was in Christ, reconciling the world unto himself, not imputing their trespasses unto them; and hath committed unto us the word of reconciliation.

2Co 5:19

Now then we are ambassadors for Christ, as though God did beseech you by us: we pray you in Christ's stead, be ye reconciled to God.

2Co 5:20

For he hath made him to be sin for us, who knew no sin; that we might be made the righteousness of God in him.

2Co 5:21

When we get saved, we are changed; we are no longer a sinner but born-again, blood-bought believers. We are reconciled back to the Father through Jesus Christ. We are redeemed, believers.

We are overcomers, we learn how to attack the enemy and we learn how to stand our ground. WE ARE CHRISTIANS.

About The Author

Samuel D Brannon was born in Tahlequah, Oklahoma Cherokee County. He was saved at 12, began to preach at 13 and was Ordained at 20 in the Free Holiness and Bishop of Gospel Time Ministries. He is now fifty and has ministered for over 30 years. He has pastored three churches and has Ministries on Facebook and YouTube. In 1991, Sam married his wife Rosa together they have one son, named Patrick. Sam and his family reside in Oklahoma.

Thank you, Rev. Sam Brannon

"Attack is Victory keep fighting"

Sam Brannon

www.ingramcontent.com/pod-product-compliance
Lightning Source LLC
Chambersburg PA
CBHW060329260626
47160CB00007B/2744
* 9 7 9 8 8 9 3 9 7 2 6 8 9 *